# a story about falling
## by
### Sarah

Don't Let Me Go

© 2015
by Sarah

All Rights Reserved

Cover Design: Sarah
Interior Design: E.M. Tippetts Book Designs

emtippettsbookdesigns.com
Editor: Karin Kempert Lawson

First Edition

Bibliographical Note:
Don't Let Me Go first appeared in Branded: A Bad Boys Anthology in 2014

*For CL,*
*love is never alone in the dark.*

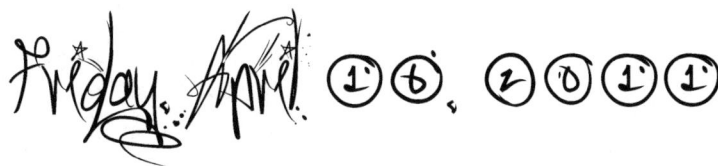

## 8:49 am

"So, we're on the couch, and this girl has a mouth like a sugar scoop made of sunshine."

"Jesus Christ. What year was it, Len?"

"1959."

"It was 1959, and I was in my prime—"

"Actor."

"Hey, cut the gas. Delores June was hot to trot."

Keeping still for my barber, Barlow's hands and a second hot towel, I laugh under my breath. I open my eyes as he removes the warmth, but I don't turn my head.

"Get to the best part," he prompts his business partner and best friend of forty-plus years, Leonard.

With hot lather brushed across my jaw, I lean back. The subtle smell of sandalwood and vanilla clings to me, mixing with the shop's scent of coffee and newsprint.

1

# Don't Let Me Go

"So everything's cooking with little Delores, and I know she's married, but her husband's out of town on business," Leonard says, his age and unfiltered cigarette-roughened voice light with pride over air conditioning that's blowing more noise than cool air. "I shouldn't be worried."

I close my eyes against early sunlight pouring in through the front windows of Aces in the Cut as Barlow makes his first pass with the straight edge. Even as my pulse puts the pedal to my ribs, I don't tense.

Not here.

Nothing reminds you you're alive like letting another man bring a blade to your throat, but I'm laid back in this place. A shave and a haircut with my own business partner and best friend of more than a decade, Josef-*Moscow*-Dolzhikov, is every other Friday morning for a few years now. It's just the four of us in the shop today, plus Sonny, who's unconcerned with his dirty brown mop top and thumbing through today's Baltimore Sun on the shoe shine bench.

Our livelihood may be shifting, but this ease remains.

"I'm not worried." Leonard clarifies. "I'm not thinking about anything but how this girl's got her lips to heaven and I'm about to make her an angel."

Sonny chuckles.

"I don't hear it when a car pulls up outside. This chump mother—" the old man pauses, huffing. "Mr. June's home a day early."

Barlow glides the blade over my chin, and as Dolzhikov's barber probably does the same to him, he snorts derisive disbelief.

"So we're on our feet, and she's flipping out, but we're not fast

2

enough. He's got the door open and he's calling for her, and I'm spry, but I'm five-four—what am I going to do with a pissed off husband?"

"Finish on his wife's face," Sonny says, sly amusement striping his tone.

It's hard not to laugh.

"I was narrowed in," Len defends. "We're on our feet in this back room, and Delores is all pink in the cheeks, a dead giveaway, but right before this guy turns the corner, my pulse just kicks me. Right in the chest. I pull my shirt up over my nose and push baby girl face down onto the same couch she was just showing me love on, and I tell this cat to kiss the fucking floor before I stomp his wife's pretty face."

Sonny scoffs, skeptical and carefree, and my boy speaks up while his man wields a razor.

"No you didn't," he says. I can hear him grinning distrustfully. "Tell the truth. You ran out the back like a pussy."

"You're damn right I did," Leonard replies like no shit. "But not until I made Mr. June empty his wallet, and he then *offered* all the savings from his safe that I could carry. I didn't finish, but I left with fucking—"

Bells clink and chime against the front door as it opens, quieting the man recounting his last minute plan. As Barlow cleans me up, I open my eyes to see three teenage boys enter. Not old enough to drive, let alone shave, they sit in chairs along the front window, flipping through comics and awaiting haircuts. Sonny drops the paper and picks up one of the two cellphones from the seat next to him, scrolling through it while Leonard returns to his work.

"When it comes down, that's how you gotta do it," he says. "All or nothing."

Sitting up, I smell like bay rum and talc, and I feel cleaner than I have in days. Barlow turns on the television in the corner for the kids, but the game is a background buzz accompanied by the old AC unit. The five of us are quiet as razors are traded for combs, and young trouble converses in harmless low tones over the pages of *Hellboy, Batman,* and *Punisher.*

As my man turns on the clippers and brings them to the back of my neck, the phone Sonny isn't scrolling through, rings. I watch as he picks it up, silences it, and sets it back down while Dolzhikov readjusts his position.

His girl's got him doing that.

Not a minute goes by before the phone rings again.

"D," Sonny says, picking it back up. "Violet."

Dolzhikov sighs before he replies, "No."

I glance between them, and the kids at the front sound off for the batter's third strike as the phone Sonny's still holding starts to ring again.

"D—"

"No, man."

Leonard pauses, hanging back while his client, the boy I came up from Baltimore's Juvenile Justice Center with, pops his knuckles under his cape and tries to shake girl-stress from shifty shoulders.

"Fuck," he cuts, frustrated under his breath. He sniffs, and it isn't because he needs to sneeze, and it sure as hell isn't because he's about to start crying.

She's got him doing that too, though.

4

# a story about falling by Sarah

My jaw tenses, and I bring my teeth together behind sealed lips.

"So," Leonard speaks lightheartedly as the lack of ringing lingers and he starts trimming again, "You're heading out to play with the unkempt masses of D.C. this weekend?"

I catch Barlow's well-weathered smile out of the corner of my eye.

"Hell yes," Sonny answers.

Leonard shakes his head.

"Bunch of long-haired ne'er-do-wells that get younger, dirtier and more pretentious by the year."

I crack a smirk.

"I'd shave 'em all," he says.

Laughing as Barlow finishes up the longer top of my hair, I stand up after he removes the cape, and dust off. In the mirror, I run my fingers through freshly soft dark brown and slide my palm down the faded smooth sides and back of my head. I meet the only color on me, hazel flecked blue eyes, and they reflect a faded black tee and holey kneed black jeans close-fitted on a frame taller than anyone I know.

"Is that your way of saying you want us to bring you back a little patchouli-dipped hippie chick?" Sonny asks from the bench.

Pulling a Jolly Rancher from my pocket, I give my impatient teeth hard sugar to appease their need.

Scissors over comb on the left side of Dolzhikov, Len scoffs.

"In your words, Sonny, hell yes."

Meeting my Ace at the counter, I pay him and shake his hand while the phone next to Sonny starts up yet again, making the shells of D's exposed ears redden.

5

"Here," I say, walking over. Grabbing the phone, I head outside and squint against surrounding sunshine. Spring wind blows warm across me as I roll my eyes at the screen, slide my thumb across it, and bring my boy's phone straight up.

"Alright, Violet," I answer, looking up and down the street, expecting an earful of angry girlfriend.

Instead, I get urgent alarm.

"Rhys is here."

My stomach drops as cars and buses roll by, and all my nerves stand on end.

"What?"

"He just left. Aster forgot her lipgloss last night. So we came to get it, and Rhys was getting in his car when we pulled up— wait. CL? Fuck you, *alright, Violet,*" she mocks. "You think I'm fucking scared of you? Put Josef on the phone—"

I pull her high-pitched highness away from my ear as Sonny opens the door with his shades on, and joins me on the sidewalk.

"What's up?" he asks with a lowered voice and raised brows.

Shaking my head, I bring the phone back up with a deep breath to hear spoiled, strung out, and real smart still ranting.

"Alright, alright, look," I interrupt. "Stay there. Don't go inside. We're coming."

Sonny's light eyes are hidden behind dark lenses, but confusion comes through in forehead wrinkles and tight lips. His brows lift further as I hang up, and a chill runs under my skin, pulling blood from the surface and sending it to muscle tissue instead with sparks of anticipation.

Lighting a cigarette the second he's outside, D squints like I did and holds his hand out to Sonny for his aviators.

"She pissed?" He sniffs as he puts them on, and passes me his car keys.

Like I didn't know he was anxious as fuck and too bent for a bump to drive.

Getting into his '66 Impala, I wish I'd have grabbed my own sunglasses this morning. I drop the visor to block some of the brightness and start the old SS while Dolzhikov gets in the passenger side. Holding his cigarette in his right hand, he takes a hit from the vial in his pocket with his left.

Violet's got him doing this shit more than ever too.

Sonny's quiet in the middle of the back seat as I turn us around and head west instead of south—toward the house in Gaithersburg and away from the party in the heart of D.C.

The candy between my back teeth is about gone, and I want something stronger for the fixation I've always carried, doubled by this morning's chemical comedown.

I want a blunt, but—

"Where are we going?" D asks.

I lean back.

"Call Rhys," I answer, turning onto South Howard.

"What?"

"Just ... See how he answers."

"Why?" Sonny asks, leaning forward with his elbows on the bench seat while D dials and listens.

Sunlight shines brighter as we head into it. The city's rising and grinding. Buses full of kids heading to their last day of school before spring break and hybrid cars on morning commutes crowd the streets, moving with us while joggers jog, and the less hasty walk their dogs. Men stroll in suits, and pigeons swoop

7

while I wait with an unsteady pulse, because this guy—

"It's off." D says, pocketing his phone. "What's going on?"

This sleazy, amoral fucking guy—Rhys—is forgetting himself, and he could knock the whole ladder out from under my boy and everything he's building, including me and Sonny.

And Baxter.

Wherever he is.

Sonny leans closer while warm wind blows in through all four rolled-down windows, and my nerves itch under my skin.

"Violet just caught him leaving Gaithersburg," I answer, merging onto 395.

Trusty and affronted ties flare the air moving through the cab of the Impala with the tension of offense. Sonny falls back, and D looks over at me.

"You want to step on the fucking gas, CL?"

## 10:14 am

"What the fuck is your problem?"

"Calm down, Violet."

"What the fuck took you so long?"

"There's traffic because of the festival."

"So? And what, you're too big to answer your own phone now?"

All big blue eyes, skinny lips, and bony hips sticking out over cut-off short-shorts, Violet takes a break from cutting up her boyfriend to shoot me the same resentful look she always does as Sonny and I get out of the car.

And I get it.

I hear what she's saying.

D's going through some growing pains.

But this shit isn't helping.

"Give it a rest," he says, flicking his cigarette as he walks toward his favorite bad habit and her lipgloss-forgetting best friend.

Closing my door as Sonny closes his, I look around our wide-open acres. Neighboring houses are few and far between, and it's late enough in the morning now that anyone with anywhere to be, already is.

D owns this house for one reason: so Violet, Aster, Hyacinth and Rose can turn powder Mandy into double and triple stacked Mollies, and stamp little crowns on the finished product.

But the two blondes posted against the trunk of his girlfriend's beat-up Monte Carlo are supposed to be off today.

We all are.

Sonny idles next to me, a few feet back from Dolzhikov and the girls. Starlings sing in the beech tree branches above us, and their songs in the otherwise spacious silence tighten my nerves. I pocket my hands for placation and ease, but every muscle between my jaw and shoulders aches, and I've only got one Jolly Rancher left to bear down on.

"Did you guys go inside?" D asks, lower now, concerned as he can be.

"No," Violet answers, lighter. "We just got here, and Rhys was pulling out of the driveway."

"Moscow, I'm sorry—" Aster starts to apologize and explain what I've already told him, but he holds his hand up.

"Stay out here," he says.

I step as he turns, and Sonny follows.

Besides the copy D recently made for his girl, he and I are the only two with keys to this place. There's no sign of a break-in as we approach the front door, but that doesn't do much for the rough influx of epinephrine and cortisol coursing through me as he unlocks it. I don't touch what's unlicensed, hidden under my shirt and double-holstered beneath my waistband as we enter, but I'm conscious of both Glock 19s on my hips as we spread out.

Nothing's missing or out of place inside the house. My duffel of savings is secure with D's in the floor safe, along with the rest of his stockpile, and all the schedule I investments in the basement are accounted for. From the looks of it, Rhys didn't get in, but none of that is the point, which remains heavy:

We're here because he wasn't supposed to be.

The ten grand Rhys owes my best friend isn't a big deal, not really, especially compared to what Moscow's made of and moving up to.

But pride is.

Shade is.

And ten thousand is only half of Rhys' debt.

That's why he was supposed to be in Panama City, working shit off when the flower girls caught him here.

But in truth, Rhys isn't the only one fucking up.

D never should have sent that guy with more than—

"So, what's going on?"

Sonny draws as he turns toward the question, but lowers his shit and walks away as the girls enter the back room we're in.

"Jesus, Violet," D barks. "Didn't I tell you to stay outside?"

"What? I have to stay in the yard like your dog or something?"

While they couple their mess out, I head back to the front with Sonny. We lean against the Impala, and when he offers me a cigarette, it's far from my first choice, but I take it. Menthol and bitter smoke do little to appease the need in me and more to give

11

me a head rush while Sonny kicks at the gravel in the driveway.

"What do you think he's doing?"

"Rhys?" I ask.

"Yeah."

I shrug, lightheaded but closing my lips around another drag.

I've known Santiago—*Sonny*—Sandoval longest. We came up from spelling bees and school plays a year before I pushed Simon Pilkington down a flight of stairs.

In fairness, I didn't mean to.

The punk fell back when my fist hit his face, but that didn't matter. Eleven years old and in court-declared need of anger management, I was sent to the detention center where ten-year-old Moscow was in for trading his sister's Adderall for dime bags from junior high kids.

Rhys didn't move to Baltimore until we were sophomores, and Baxter didn't transfer here until we were seniors.

I'm not as quick to fly off the handle as I used to be, but Dolzhikov?

He's only moved up in the barter system.

Chesapeake Bay's biggest street dealer, working his way to MDMA middle-man for the entire east coast gets along more than fine in light of what Rhys owes him, and the deal he sent him on in Florida obviously went through, or we'd have heard from Nemoy by now.

I know pride is a bitch to swallow, but D needs to fucking cut this guy loose.

The front door opens as I flick what's left of Sonny's cigarette, and my boy comes out holding his girl's hand. Smiling up into his cheeks under his sunglasses, fresh haircut all sex-fucked-up,

12

# a story about falling by Sarah

he looks a little younger and more himself. Just as short as Violet, and as blond as the light coming through the trees, my brother in all this is as loose as can be in his walk.

All of this bullshit aside, that's what he is to me. He doesn't need to justify a thing.

We go back too far for that.

"What are we waiting for?" he asks, tucking conceited but complacent into her car with a smirk.

My head's dizzy, and my mouth tastes like burnt settling, but my heart thumps steadily behind my ribs as D strides toward the passenger side of his '66, grinning at me over the roof of it.

"Let's go get this motherfucker."

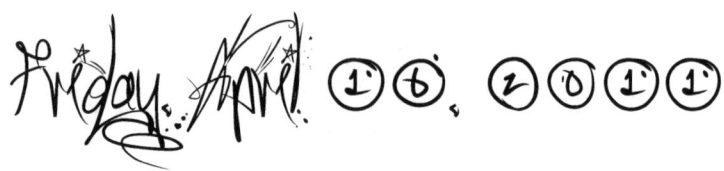

## 1:44 pm

"I'm tired."

"Dude."

"Can we get some more coffee?"

"Man, let it go."

"D and CL had me up early."

"Eight o'clock isn't exactly early, Sonny."

"Yeah, bitch," Bax agrees snidely. "If you had a job—"

"What?" Sonny returns. "You mean besides dicking your mom full-time?"

"Yeah? Is that what you're doing when I'm taking Anarosa out for ice cream?"

Joking toes the line this close to disrespect, and I don't have to look from the road to the back seat to know Bax probably grabbed his business when he said it, as if mentioning Sonny's little sister's crush on him wasn't enough.

14

Sonny hits his arm, and Baxter hits back, but they're laughing. Neither of them are exactly faithful to their girlfriends, but it's a given.

Sisters are different.

Love and loyalty run deep between us, but there's no way in hell I'd let them that kind of near to Lydie.

Between tight teeth and commotion in the back seat, I almost laugh.

Turning the SS onto North Broadway with the heel of my right hand, I make myself sit straighter. While I don't agree that eight a.m. is early, my body's burdened with tired.

Rolling all night on the purest ecstasy around when I was seventeen was one thing, but six years makes an intense difference.

I crashed on D's couch, counting on sleeping all day and heading to the festival tonight, but my boy was up with the sun, and now there's all this shit with Rhys.

Setting my left elbow on the window's edge, I rest the back of my head in my palm. In the rearview, Sonny and Bax scan the sidewalks out separate sides while a line of cars cruises steadily behind us. It's the same in front of me. People are everywhere, and it wears on already present pressure.

We've been all over the city.

Rhys' apartment.

His girlfriend's apartment.

His friends' shitty apartments.

His peon fucking job.

The salon his girl works at.

His parents' house.

But if this guy's crazy enough to be in Gaithersburg when he's supposed to be halfway from Florida to here, he's already gone. Maybe not from Baltimore, because his girl was at work and he's not leaving her, but Rhys has long checked the fuck out of his head.

We're not going to find him, because that's the thing about finding a maniac.

You don't.

The more daylight we burn, that fact only gains weight. It twists and digs deeper between all of us and into my patience. Two o'clock becomes three, and three strings itself into four. Sonny isn't the only one who's hungry anymore, but futile frustration keeps us quiet while Nas' *Illmatic* bass line thumps hard through the speakers. Even with the windows down and the sun still up, the growing magnitude of being in the dark stifles and provokes.

My fuse is the longest it's ever been, but anxiety's a pusher and next to me, Dolzhikov's feeling it twice as hard. His temper all but radiates in the pause between "Memory Lane" and "One Love".

"He's probably out of town by now." Sonny speaks up, breaking the silence no music fills with what none of us wants to say. "He'll be back."

"Like I don't fucking know that?" D clips over his shoulder. He turns the stereo off and stretches his legs. He sits up. He leans back, nervous, and he shakes his head, craving.

Driving with my knee, I pull the last Jolly Rancher from my pocket and unwrap it.

"If he's desperate enough to be fucking around when he ain't even supposed to be back yet..." Dolzhikov turns to face Sonny,

16

# a story about falling by Sarah

but leaves that thought incomplete for a new one. "He knows where you live. He knows where your girl lives. He knows where your mom and abuelita live, man, and where Anarosa goes to school. You want him laying low out there?"

Silence infolds with resentment. I press hard candy to the roof of my mouth and bear yearning up to it with a tight jaw.

I hate that they're both right.

We need to find Rhys, but driving all over the land of pleasant fucking living isn't going to just magically turn him up.

And on top of that—

"What about Hudson?" I ask, turning onto East Oliver.

A rung above Moscow in the trade and our real reason for going to D.C. this weekend, Hudson is my boy's step up, but he doesn't look over when I mention him.

"I don't know."

We're quiet again as I turn onto Ensor, putting the sun back in my eyes.

Traffic's lighter on this end of town, but the neighborhood is as busy as everywhere else with passersby. Family members dressed in mourning carry memorial wreaths into Greenmount Cemetery on our left, and to our right couples walk hand in hand while individuals pass them on casual bike rides. Two teenagers roll by on boards, and a lone brunette strides intently, like she's walking off steam.

While the scent of funeral flowers blows through the cab, grey and white headstones blur by in my peripheral, and my best friend sits straighter in his seat.

"Hey …" He nods ahead, and I follow his sight. "Look."

Sonny and Bax sit up too, focusing on the bathed-in-sunlight

17

brunette maybe three hundred feet up. In an oversized white tee and tiny denim cutoffs over sheer black tights, she's got Docs on her feet and her hands buried in her pockets. Her steps fall hard and quick, and the bottom back of her shirt says *L.A.M.B.* in bold black cursive, and I realize—

"Is that Rhys' sister?" Bax asks.

"Roll up," Moscow tells me, sinking down in his seat and turning the stereo back on low.

Looking around the block, I shift my right hand to the top of the wheel.

"She's not going to know where he is," I say under my breath.

I feel D look at me.

Swallowing the beat of hesitation from my throat, I press what's left of placating candy to the back of my teeth and cruise steadily up on the girl who's more than a mile from her parents' house. Eyes forward, I slow down as we approach her, and my passenger in his own car rolls down his window.

"Hey," he says.

From the corner of my eye, I see her turn her head.

"Hey," she answers, continuing her steps.

I cruise slower, watching cyclists and couples still passing around us. My chest fills with the fight between my conscience and my loyalty, while the resentment I carry for this girl's tweaked-out lunatic of a brother doubles up.

"You remember me?" D asks, lifting his sunglasses to the top of his head.

There's a pause, and I match her pace.

"Yeah," she tells him. "Moscow."

My stomach twists.

18

*How could she not?*

We spent more time in high school at the Sandovals' than we did anywhere else, but I remember seeing her when we'd go by to pick up Rhys, teasing her about training wheels and staying up past her bedtime.

Kennedy.

*Kenny.*

She's a kid.

"Where you heading?" D continues, voice so smooth you'd never know anything was anywhere even close to fucked.

"Um, Veronica's. My friend's house." There's uncertainty in her tone, but no fear. "We're supposed to go to D.C. but my parents grounded me this morning. Hence the long walk."

I want to swallow again, but my jaw's too tense. Not only is alone on foot undaunted, but she sounds almost emboldened by the car full of crooks creeping beside her.

"Oh, yeah? For the festival?"

The sound of my best friend's grin makes me want to gun it, but I steady my foot on the pedal, and loosen my palm against the wheel.

"Yeah."

Sunlight's blinding for a second, and she's smiling now. I can hear it. Her voice is lighter, easier, sweet as the breeze sticking to me.

I flex my fingers to keep them from tensing up.

"C'mon," D says to her, patting my right arm. "We'll give you a ride."

Keeping my eyes on the road, I slow to a stop.

Bax opens his door and gets out to let this innocent get in,

_Don't Let Me Go_

and nothing—not the tightness behind my ribs, not the piece under my buckle, not the grudge on my shoulders that I want to work into my fists and bank her piece-of-shit brother straight with—nothing is heavier on me than the sincere gratitude in this kid's tone.

"Thanks."

20

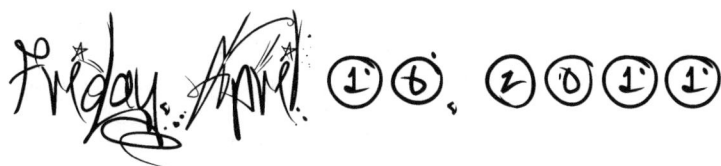

**5:16 pm**

"Wait, just for weed?"

"For like, half a little baby roach."

"That's fucked-up."

"Right?"

"They took your car?"

"And your phone?" Bax asks.

"And my laptop," the slow ride with dark eyes that I won't mistake catching again answers. In the middle of the back seat, she laughs. It's cynical, but artless, genuine, and my heart drops beats that bottom my stomach out.

"But then they left and like ... Did they really think I wasn't going to split the first chance I got?"

She sighs.

I don't look, but there's a blur of motion in the rearview as she pushes her hair back.

"It's whatever. I mean, my parents … It's not really about me anyway," she adds with less bite. "You know?"

Rolling a blunt, D nods without turning to face her.

"Yeah," he says. "Brothers are like that sometimes."

I keep my body still and my eyes on the road. The kid said her friend lives off Conway, and we're heading that direction, but when we get to the intersection and I keep straight instead of turning right, what then?

"Hey, is Williams still teaching Earth Science?" Sonny asks instead of what's weighing on all our minds.

She laughs again. "Yes."

"Dude," Sonny joins her. "That guy is so weird. Does he still start every class with *things that make you go hmm?*"

"Yes! He came in the other day talking about what your sleeping position says about you as a person."

Sonny jeers, lighthearted at home next to a pretty girl.

"He just wants to better imagine the drill team in bed," she continues. "It's so weird."

"Right? I remember one time …"

My oldest friend keeps going, and I press the heels of my restless hands against the wheel. The kid eats the attention up because we're her brother's friends. She knows us, but she doesn't *know* us, and bonds that are thicker than blood don't change the fact that the last thing this girl needs is a degenerate like Sonny making her laugh, or a street czar like Moscow getting her high. Dregs like Bax have no place near such clean hands, and I shouldn't be driving her anywhere but straight back to her parents' house.

As I approach where I'm supposed to turn and leave the

22

blinker untouched, there's a pause in nostalgic conversation. Silence dense with doubt and bass drops my stomach lower still, and when I stop at the sign only to keep straight, the smallest sound breaks the lull.

"Um …"

Surrounded by at least five guns and who's counting how many felonies, the lamb in the back seat sits up, pointing to the street I passed.

"She lives off Conway. Back there."

Uncertainty I haven't heard since we first rolled up chills her voice a few degrees, and as we get out from under neighborhood trees and onto a busier street, sunlight burns between buildings, backlighting old Sauconys hanging from a power line, right into my eyes.

I turn left to get out of its glare.

"She's probably at the festival already," D says simply, sealing the blunt. "We can find her when we get there."

He turns up the music and lights the cigar as I look around South Greene. In the wrong place at the worst time sits back, but her hesitation is unavoidable. While Nas and Damien Marley sing about patience, I strain for it.

Consciously shutting my head off, I drive, but ignoring my nerves isn't easy. Two deep lungfuls of smoke help, but don't solve anything. Like my boy, I have trouble sitting still while we figure shit out. That's part of why we drove all morning, and why we're still driving now.

I pass the blunt behind me to Sonny, who puffs twice before passing it to the kid.

If she's nervous to hit it, she's more nervous not to, because she does, and by the time it's back in the front seat, Sonny's talking again like the last few minutes never happened. Dank OG diesel and honey-dipped tobacco smoke blows around us, increasing and enforcing a vibe I've never felt. The breeze coming in is cool, but there's sweat on the back of my neck where hair would stand up if it wasn't just cut. Swells of regret and panic fuse with waves of tension and resentment, permeated with anticipation and blurred with euphoria.

In one second, my anxiety's exhilarating, and in the next, it's suffocating.

Everything becomes stifled adrenaline.

Minutes drift, but it feels like longer.

I focus on driving, but I don't know where the fuck we're going, and as I pass our last chance to merge onto the freeway toward the capital, a surge of fear from the back seat makes my hard-beating heart pound so deep, it swallows me like a current.

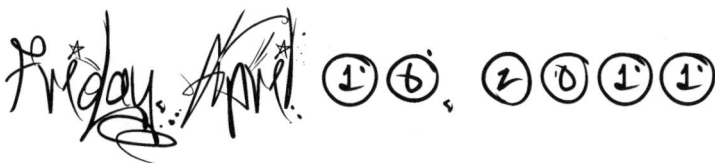

## 5:46 pm

"How're you guys doing today?"

"This party's gonna be so fucking sick."

"Last weekend—"

"Can I help you find anything?"

"Yeah, the G-spot."

"You sell cigars here too?"

The inside of Total Wine is packed with already intoxicated twenty-somethings on their way to D.C. and ragged employees just trying to do their jobs. It's unapologetically fluorescent and too crowded, but we here we are.

Standing up and walking is good for my bearings, but my pulse won't cut the pounding, and leaving the kid in the car, even though Sonny's with her, does the opposite of help.

With Bax behind me and Moscow to my left, we head down an aisle of burgundies and bordeaux that no one else is interested

25

in. I glance at my boy, about to ask him what the fuck we're doing when he looks up and speaks first.

"Take her to Six Sheets."

"What?"

"Why not?"

Stoned and loyal, but not stupid, I look right at him and lower my voice.

"You want to go the bar we launder drug money through with a fucking hostage?"

"She's not a hostage—"

"No?"

Baxter hangs back, silent, pretending interest in pinot whatthefuckever.

"Man, calm down, CL." Moscow laughs as he turns from me to the bottles. He rubs the back of his neck, shrugging.

I look over the aisle at the row of cashiers.

It's not like we haven't been in deep shit before, and it's not like our bar isn't safe, but when we're dealing or partying or being whatever kind of careless and stupid just because, it's not like this. There are things we do in the dark strictly because they're illegal, because we don't want to go to jail, but there are certain lines you don't cross.

And this—

"We gotta take her somewhere," D says easily, nudging a bottle with the toe of his red Saucony low-pro.

I fucking hate this.

"Rhys is never going to face up without a reason, and it has to be on our terms, where we say," he continues. "You know that."

I look away from him to burn my stare into a bottle of Heavy

Seas, failing over and over to understand how this person—this girl that may be a minor—isn't a hostage.

"She's a kid," I whisper.

"She left," he replies coolly. "She doesn't even have a phone. Her parents are going to think she fucking ran away. All we have to do is hang out with her somewhere and wait for Rhys to get the message. I'll tell him to bring his chick. She can take Kenny, and we can work out what we need to work out."

"Yeah, but his phone's not on," Bax speaks up in a matched hush.

"So we'll fucking call the salon and tell his bitch, you'll never guess who says hi." Moscow looks from him to me like it's simple. "We'll be done in time to get to D.C. tonight. We just need a place."

His nonchalance does nothing for the tight-sick twist in my stomach or the pressure in my chest, while his half-cocked plan does everything to put us back where we started. Scanning the store and combing our collective possibilities, we're wordless as people pass us, until the guy who's almost my height, with a fuse half as short as mine used to be, speaks up.

"It's cool," Bax says. Suntanned under dark hair and even darker eyes, he drops his hand onto my shoulder. I look at him, and he looks at Dolzhikov. "I know somewhere we can go."

"Yeah?" D asks.

"Yeah, it's in Brookland. They won't ask questions."

My instincts push me to avoid any place Baxter goes where they don't ask questions, but as they walk, I follow.

You don't turn your back on your friends.

On our way out, D picks up a pack of peach Optimos and a

six pack of Small Craft as Bax grabs two bottles of Jager. While they pay, I set down a bag of Jolly Ranchers and don't hesitate to ask the clerk for a bottle of Blue Label.

"Special occasion?" short, shifty-shouldered and running the show asks, brows lifted as he looks up from his phone.

I split a smile as I step back to let him shell out a few hundreds for the top shelf scotch. It won't change where we are, but I'm doing this for him.

"Yeah," I answer. "You fucking owe me."

Back in the car, the blunt's out.

Sonny and the kid sit in stressed silence.

The scent of clean flowers and grapefruit that I've been ignoring since she first got in hits me stronger as I sit back down, but I don't look.

We're doing this and getting it over with.

That's it.

As I head southwest toward Brookland, Bax passes Sonny a bottle while D opens his. Tucking mine under the seat, I unwrap a Jolly Rancher because my jaw is more in need than my nerves as we merge onto the freeway. The second it's between my teeth though, I feel worse instead of better, because we didn't get our reason for stopping anything.

What if she's hungry?

Or thirsty?

I bet her nerves could use at least a double.

Burning up US 50, I glance in the rearview. I'm checking for cars, but dark eyes find mine. It's just for a second, but the desperation she's holding down has her pupils so wide, everything between my ribs freezes and sinks to my stomach.

## a story about falling by Sarah

When she speaks, her quailing isn't nearly as hidden as she probably hopes.

"Where are we going?"

I pull the bottle out from under my seat.

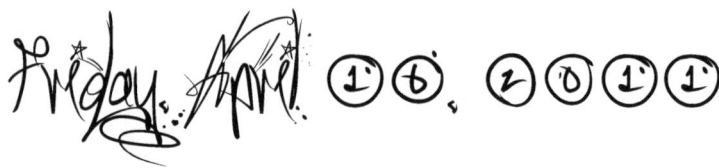

Friday, April 16, 2011

## 6:34 pm

"Bax, you limp dick motherfucker!"

"Robinson, how's it going, man?"

"Come here, come on inside. You guys here for the festival?"

"You know it."

"What's up, guys?"

We're just parked and out of the car when this scraggly hippie stubs out his cigarette on the side of the business that's apparently his own. Baxter leads the way. D follows him, holding his hand out to me for his car keys. I pass them over, and when he turns around to tell the kid, "C'mon," I fall in behind her with Sonny beside me.

With a bloodstream flowing premium scotch and a bad feeling, and sunlight burning my shoulders through my black cotton, all I can think is, of course Bax brought us here. There are

30

bars on the windows and no light shining from inside.

Approaching the entrance, I check out the pawn shops, payday loan dealers, and Chinese restaurants that make up the rest of the run-down strip mall. I take in dandelions growing up from cracked cement and the careless way *Executive Lounge* looks hand-painted on the chipped stucco front of our safe place.

I look any and everywhere but at the black lettering across the small of the back in front of me.

Inside the hole in the wall, it's no better.

It's dark. It's dirty. It smells like sweat, bleach, and the scent that lingers from running an old vacuum. Static-crackled music plays from somewhere above us, but it's hard to make out much more than warped guitars and tribal drums.

There's a few people at the bar and tables, and even though none of them are concerned with any of us, everything inside me says bail.

"This is the man," Bax tells the burnout at least a few years our senior. He turns and pats D on the shoulder. "Moscow, this is Robinson."

Colored red and blue by dim neon Coors and Budweiser lights, Dolzhikov extends his hand.

"Good to meet you. 'Snice place."

Tall, devious and tie-dyed under the same lights as the rest of us, the owner smirks.

"It gets the job done."

My skin crawls.

Smirking with him, D sniffs. It's faultless in itself. I know his vial's empty and he's feeling it, but between that sound and the teenager between us with her head down, we probably look like

31

we need somewhere to do some filthy fucking dirt. If this were my place, I'd be suspicious, not welcoming.

"Make yourselves at home. Let me get you guys drinks."

We sit at a rickety table, the kid between D and me, and Robinson brings us drafts that taste like gutter water. Bax smokes a cigarette, easy in this element, while on my left, Sonny checks out the other customers. Relaxing back, not too uncomfortable anywhere, he seems like he could make this place work for why we're here, but Moscow doesn't lean. He sits up straight, lips tight and lids low over skeptical eyes.

I don't look to my right, but I know from peripheral sight the girl's barely sitting on the edge of her seat, palpably still. Dread free-flows from her, making my already unstable heart beat harder and feeding D's unease, which further perpetuates my own.

"So …" Robinson returns, pulling up a chair. "What's up, man? How's life? How's Charlotte?"

I speak up before Bax can answer.

"You have somewhere we can go?" I ask, brushing my nose with my thumb when the owner looks over.

He points behind us as an answer, and his dilated eyes land on the person who's too young to be in here. I stand up in his line of sight.

Sonny and D rise too, and as my oldest friend turns to find and lead our way, my closest nudges the kid's shoulder. She stands, and I step aside to let her walk in front of me. Trepidation pours heavier from her with every step, but none of us push or hold on to the girl who's become a ransom, and I don't understand why she doesn't at least try to run.

## a story about falling by Sarah

The Executive Lounge is longer than it looks from the outside, and its greasy clientele glance as we pass. Every set of eyes feels like a rope around my chest, making everything between my ribs throb with compressed pressure. I've stepped in something that makes both of my Vans stick with every stride, and by the time Sonny finally opens a door, every nerve I've got needles me to do something.

He flips a switch that illuminates a bare bulb as we file into a room with a threadbare love seat, crates of paperwork, and open boxes of old clothes. It's stuffy, musty, and cramped, but drier than the rest of the place. A Pink Floyd poster hangs on the far wall, in between an open bathroom door in the corner and another door that leads outside.

"No lock?" Dolzhikov asks as Sonny messes with each of the handles.

He shakes his head in response, and we stand in a sort of circle with Rhys' sister on my right, Sonny next to her, and my impulsive prick of a best friend across from me. All eyes wait on him, except the scared pair staring holes into my shoes.

"Did you text him?" Sonny asks.

"Yeah."

"Nothing?"

"No."

"Fuck."

Under the sound of distorted funk-metal beats and the weight of what the fuck are we doing, I just listen.

"What do we do?" Sonny continues.

Like what he's talking about isn't silently freaking out right next to him.

33

"Hey," Bax says, knocking on the other side of the door before he opens it. Falling right into our circle, he repeats Sonny's question. "Nothing?"

D shakes his head, scanning the room and silencing an incoming phone call.

I press my hands into my pockets while sweat drags down the back of my neck, turning into chills that slither under my collar and creep across my back. Swallowing takes too much effort, and the kid's dread has escalated to terror so thick, it fucks with every one of my breaths.

"I mean, how long are we supposed to wait?" Sonny asks.

"I don't know." D shrugs, checking a text. "Maybe this guy's got a basement or something."

Pressure drops to pure vertigo.

"Sonny," my boy continues, pocketing his phone. "Go keep Robinson busy."

The second the door closes behind him, stale air thins further, and Bax shifts his feet.

"Should we tie her up?"

My right hand comes out of my pocket to cover my mouth and rub my chin, and I have to look away because she looks up, dark eyes darting between the three of us.

It all happens way too fast.

The last thing I see before the rush is the writing on the poster across from us.

*Wish You Were Here.*

In a blur of grabbing and pushing and stumbling past me, Bax covers her mouth and picks her up, her struggle knocking off his old school Orioles hat while Moscow heads toward the bathroom that's more like a closet. He pulls a string attached to the ceiling, and a black light shines on everything as Bax drags the kid in, his all white Nikes glowing brighter than the floor.

"Over there," he says, nodding to a box while the kid screams behind his hand and tears at his arms.

Rifling through old clothes, D passes Bax a scarf for her mouth and grabs more, pushing them into my hands.

Used silk weighs a thousand pounds.

"Tie her," he tells me, stepping back.

Strained and muffled screams freeze my bloodstream as I glance from what's undeniably become kidnapping to my best friend, and just in case the fury in his all-pupil eyes doesn't say it all—

"Like I need to explain how fucked we are if she gets away now? Tie her, CL."

Pushed onto her side and held down under Bax and black light, she shakes her head fiercely against the tiles. Horrified dark eyes rip wider open, tears streaming as she screams harder. Even under the scarf, it's deafening, and I lose it.

My gut kicks me right in the chest, and I move like a heart attack.

She fights like hell on the tiles, hitting and then kicking as I tie her hands first, then bind her elbows to her sides. The heel of her boot splits my temple when I reach for her legs, but I don't say anything, and I don't look up as I pin her to the floor. Holding her efforts under my knee, I tie her ankles, and she screams pleading cries, urgent and hopeless and broken-rough in her throat.

Deaf and blind and inundated, I don't hear the door open behind me, just the sound of her quick silence, guns drawn and

35

Sonny's shock.

"Whoa, what the fuck—"

Adrenaline rips through me as I stand up. Closing the door, I lock myself in front of it, and stifled little cries echo through old wood while my pulse throttles my eardrums.

"What the fuck are you guys doing?" Sonny asks, eyes gaping as he steps forward, and Bax and Moscow put their shit away.

"Didn't I tell you to keep Robinson busy? What's he doing?"

"He doesn't care, man. He's got some rat in his lap. What the fuck is this?"

D's phone rings again, and he silences the call to send another text, and I already know.

I know it before he says anything.

"Just fucking stay put," he tells all of us, unclipping his keys from his belt loop.

I don't move, but my sense of brotherhood and family, the place in my heart where inviolable devotion lives, thinks twice.

Is this how far back we go?

Would he do this if I asked?

Is that what friendship is? I love you and I've got you, but only as far as you've got me?

"Where are you going?" Sonny asks.

"I'll be back."

"When? I mean—"

"I have to make some fucking calls, alright? Stay put."

Moscow's out the back door just like that, and I know it's for his habits—the empty one in his pocket and the other one he already filled this morning—but understanding doesn't make any part of this any easier.

# a story about falling by Sarah

The small screams behind me have given way to sobs. Breathing in, I'm dizzy. I close my eyes for a second, but all I see are hers. Wide and wet, red under dirty pale purple light, that look isn't ever going to leave me, and I know it. However this plays out, this shit's with me for life.

Is that what friendship is?

Opening my eyes as I breathe out, I turn around.

"What are you doing?" Bax asks as I open the door. "CL, what the fuck are you doing?"

Deep and sweeping dark eyes fasten to me, and she flinches as I kneel, but I hold my palms up for a second of promise before I reach for the scarf covering her mouth. Unmuzzled, she gasps hard, hauling breaths so frantic and unmanageable they move her entire torso, but she doesn't scream, and for a second I'm overwhelmed with the smell of citrus and wet metal.

She freezes compliantly as I reach for her hands, but her entire frame shakes. I don't look anywhere I don't have to as I unbind her wrists and arms, but pangs of disappointment and guilt course violently through me when I pull silk away to reveal red marks that too-tight knots leave behind.

As I shift to free her ankles, darkness slides and drips into my right eye. I wipe away blood she shed with the back of my hand as I stand again.

"You heard what D said about her getting away," Sonny half-warns, half-worries.

"Does it look like she's trying to get away?" I reply, swiping my red hand on my black jeans and stepping away from the bathroom. "She wasn't trying to run in the first place."

In the corner of my eye, untied and still trembling sits sort of timidly up, keeping herself bent and low as she rubs away tears and cradles her wrists.

"So what?" Bax says, reproach rough in his tone.

Looking around and between my friends, I repocket my hands.

"Can't we just chill out?" Sonny questions. "He's probably calling Rhys right now."

"You know where he is?" Bax asks.

I don't realize he's addressing the kid, and I don't think she does either until he says, "Hey," and she looks up from foot-level.

The backs of my eyes, my sinuses, everything in me stings.

I run drugs.

That's what I do.

I make and move enough methylenedioxy-methylamphetamine across the East Coast to get me ten to life straight off the bat, no questions asked. I've seen and done things in the past five years I'll take to the dirt, but I've never felt more criminal than I do looking at this kid on the floor, coated in ultraviolet.

"No," she says quietly. "Sorry."

Throwing his hands in the air, Sonny turns around.

"This is fucking stupid," he says while Bax shakes his head, and I watch without a word. "All I wanted was to fuck some hippie chicks, eat some fucking half-smokes, step up, and come home. Now we've got this fucking hostage—"

"She's not a hostage."

"Are you out of your mind?"

"Just let D get straight, alright."

"He doesn't know what the fuck he's doing." Sonny gestures

in mine and the innocent's direction like evidence. "He's spun."

"So what? You wanna go?"

"He took the car, Einstein. And even if he didn't, how are we supposed to get laid when we're fucking babysitting?"

"Shit happens."

"Yeah, bullshit."

The tension in my jaw tightens up in their pause, all of us unsure, pissed off, and racking our brains.

"Can't we just let her go?" Sonny asks, hopeful at the end of his rope.

"Are you out of *your* mind?" Bax turns.

"What? Like she's going to say anything? Kenny, are you—"

"Don't fucking talk to her, Sonny. Where's your head at? Where's your heart?"

Their pause stretches longer this time, and I hate standing here, questioning my own loyalties.

"It's okay," our biggest problem's little sister speaks up tentatively. "My brother's an idiot." She swallows. "I don't want to be any trouble. For anybody."

Whether it's fear or truth speaking through this girl, it makes her keep stopping to handle the waver it puts in her voice.

"I won't try to run anywhere," she says lowly. "You can lock me in here."

Frustration, anger, and exasperation come up from my chest and out of me like a scoff. I shake my head as I step toward her. She doesn't shrink away when I kneel this time, but her apprehension remains thicker than the brittle air.

I look at dirty grout between the tiles instead of her face, and this time when I reach out the same hand that just tied and untied her, I grab her arm and tug her to stand up. I let go as soon as she's on her feet, while inside, my heart pounds hindsight-heightened, stress-laced, not-to-be-fucked with beats, and I look from one friend to the other.

"We're not locking her in a fucking bathroom."

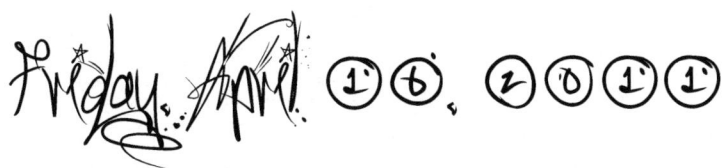

## 8:22 pm

ohnny Cash."

   "Hank Williams."

   "Sam Cooke."

"Wait. E, right?"

"E."

"Fuck …"

Sonny leans back in his chair, sipping cheap beer, as stumped as we are stuck.

I didn't want to play, but Sonny can't take too much silence and he's good at easing tension. When Bax returned to the bar, Sonny got chairs and drinks for me, himself, and the kid.

And not wanting to waste the purple urkel he brought for the weekend, he rolled a joint.

"Come on," I say around a hit. "E is so easy."

Mostly quiet and basically relaxed on my right, small and

41

Don't Let Me Go

stranded with us doesn't play along, but she sort of smiles.

"E's hard, man. Eminem and Elton John are still alive … Does Elvira count?"

Laughing at Sonny thinking the *Mistress of the Dark* could be a dead rock star makes it hard to hold smoke in. Blowing my hit toward the cobwebbed ceiling, I pass the joint right. Lamb's drank as much from her watered down cup as I have from mine, which is none at all, but she puffs twice before passing to Sonny.

"I don't think Elvira's her real name," I tell him. "And I'm pretty sure she's still alive."

"Fuck," he says again.

I'm not looking, but in the corner of my eye in this dusty-dank little room, the kid pushes her hands through her hair like girls do when they want to pull it up. She exhales smoke and brings her legs up in the fold-out chair, crossing them beneath herself.

Not like she's nervous.

But like she's okay here.

After a few seconds of honest but exaggerated obliviousness, Sonny shakes his head.

"This shouldn't be so hard," he says.

Free to laugh a little does so, and the sound of it has opposing effects. My nerves bow a bit, calmed, and I want to apologize for what I did—what we're still doing—and yet, at the same time, my muscles all contract and stretch because she's letting her guard down.

"It isn't," she says, and I almost look over for the first words she's said since thank you, when Sonny brought her a chair.

"It's so simple. It's literally *easy*."

42

"You wanna jump in now?" he playfully challenges her. "Just like that?"

"Can I?" she asks, a hint of hope in her timid tone.

I feel her glance at me, but it's quick, and I won't look over. We're still just getting this done and that's it. It's just taking longer than expected.

"You could have jumped in anytime," he tells her, passing me the joint. "Come on, what's so easy about it?"

"E," she says obviously. "Easy-E."

With a half-groan that says he should have known, Sonny covers his grin, and I can't help chuckling before I pull a hit.

"Wait," he says. "So now I have E again?"

She nods, and the way she laughs makes my shoulders square, my arms tense, and the rest of my body want to lean into the sound.

"Fuck," Sonny says a third time, downing the rest of his beer and reaching for hers like he'll find the answer in flat Natty Boh.

"Well, wait. Unless that makes it your turn?"

She looks at me again, and between smoke-clouded worries and wishing D wouldn't have left with both my appeasements still in the front seat, I almost meet her eyes.

I pass her the joint instead, and reach for the cup sitting between my Vans.

"Elvis Presley," I say evenly.

It's room temperature and anything but good, but the beer gives my eyes and hands something to do, and distracts the unabated craving in my mouth.

Sonny throws his hands up, tossing the empty cup behind him and onto the floor in defeat.

"Don't let me no" (handwritten)

"Y? So, now I have Y?"

It's hard not laugh, and as we start a new game because Yoko Ono's still alive, it's not like this is where I want to be, but pressure fading—even just temporarily—makes room for weird hope.

My boy's been gone longer than I'd like, but long enough that at this point, maybe it's because shit's getting handled. Rhys is a fuck-up, but he always lands on his feet by the skin of his teeth. Maybe we can still all go our separate ways before midnight.

But I don't hold my breath, and as minutes pass into an hour and another game ends, anticipation and regret are back to tightening my chest like there's a prize for it.

Sonny brings in two more drinks. I shake my head, but the kid takes hers, and I feel just like I did in the car. My heart beats back and forth between frustration and a buzz, and while the two of them talk about rolling another joint, I wonder where the nearest Metro stop is, and if I could put her on a bus before D gets back.

I'm unpocketing my phone to find out when I hear the Impala roll up outside.

As soon as Dolzhikov opens the back door, alone, fear from my right fleeces all of me, and every skinny hope that this could get any kind of better dissipates.

"What's going on?" His eyes are almost all pupil and when he sniffs, my hands tense. "Are you guys ready?"

I want to fucking light him up.

Everywhere that wondering was, everywhere in me that disquiet and dedication have been warring, fills with annoyance, because I get it.

I do.

**44**

# a story about falling by Sarah

This whole situation has been fucked since before this morning, but *this*—

Stranding us here like ducks so he can get blown—

"Ready for what?" I ask, biting defiance.

My boy shifts on his feet, looking around the room. A stretched out shirt and push-pulled hair attest to a fuck or two, but the lack of smirking, boyish pride proves it wasn't Violet.

"D.C." he states.

The vibe around us goes from a meager lingering semblance of lax to ridiculously uncomfortable. Bax enters without a word. Sonny and still cross-legged but no longer at ease on my right remain silent, while fed-up impatience bitters the back of my tongue.

"What about the kid?"

"What about her?" Turning his back, blond and bombed lights a cigarette and thumbs absentmindedly through a crate of paperwork. "Leave her with Robinson. We got better shit to do."

There's a foot or so of concrete floor space between me and the girl, but her panic, electric and clinging, covers me. My own reluctance runs a chill under my skin and my blood shrinks back from it. I'm about to say alright, let's fucking take her home then, but it's Sonny who speaks up.

"D, Lindsay's been texting me."

Moscow turns around.

"Pussy," he taunts.

"You know how it is," Sonny fibs. He hasn't looked at his phone once. "She's pissed I didn't invite her."

"Fine. Whatever. I'm still going. Violet's meeting us there."

New bullshit aside, the dark eyed predicament on my right

45

remains petrified.

"What about the girl?" Bax asks.

"I don't fucking care, man." D gestures between her and where she was he left. "What's all this shit anyway?"

"We're not locking her in a bathroom," I say a second time, sitting straighter, meeting his coke-confidence head-on without standing yet.

"Fine."

The corners of his mouth curve carelessly up as my boy shrugs. His dope-shifty eyes glint under bare-bulb light while he drags from his cigarette and looks at me for the first time since he arrived.

The plan he came here with becomes crystal clear before he says it.

"You don't want to keep her in there?" he asks without wanting an answer.

What I know is coming hits my stomach like a shot. Acid anger seethes in my throat and the impulse to shove control doubles up, familiar and consciously hard to resist.

"Cool," he says, blowing smoke. "She can stay here with you."

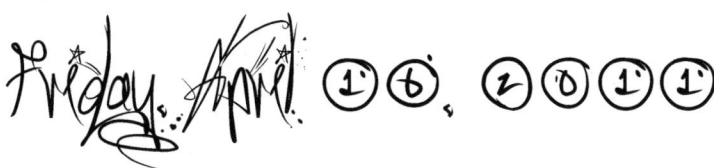

## 10:08 pm

"Two more bombs, man."

"Your fucking mother."

"I said pray to God."

"Sheila, where's the E?"

"Ice, man! We need ice!"

In the black-lit bathroom with the door closed, shouts and neo-groove guitar riffs that have only gotten louder as the bar filled up muffle through thin walls. I bring another palmful from the cold tap up to my face and the back of my neck.

It steadies me.

But just for a second.

I shut off the faucet, and water drips from my chin and the hoop in my nose as I turn around and bring my tee shirt up. The cut in my eyebrow stings as I rub over it and dry the rest of my face. I close my eyes to clear my head, but it reels and I wish the kid would take the opportunity to get out before it gets any worse.

When my friends split, I left my responsibility in her chair so I could pull my shit together.

But I know she's going to be there when I open the door again.

And as hard as I resign everything else inside me, there's this sinking feeling I can't shut down.

My jaw tenses, and I dig my teeth into my bottom lip.

Blinking damp lashes, I run my hands down my face and push my hair back, taking a deep breath in through my nose before opening the door.

I glance only quickly enough to find the lamb still in her chair, just like I knew she would be. She looks up as I look away, and the sinking feeling in my gut pulls from between my shoulders, down through my chest and deeper into my stomach.

Not glancing back at her or the room as I speak, I head toward our exit.

"Come on."

Outside, nighttime is cloudlessly cool. The open air alleviates some of anxiety's thick oppression, and I heard the kid follow, but she doesn't ask where we're going. She catches up with quick, uneven boot steps as I round the corner from 13th to Hamlin, heading toward the traffic I can see down on 12th. While she could easily turn and run, she keeps herself almost beside me instead.

I rub my eyes and pick up my pace.

12th NE isn't as packed as it could be with the festival just a few miles away, but cars cruise by and businesses' fluorescents light the drunk, poor, and already spring-broken. A bus passes on the opposite side of the street, and I stop in front of Silvestre Cafe.

The air stinks like rotisserie chicken, burnt gas, and black powder.

"Alright," I say, looking around. "There's Metro stops up and down this block."

Bass and violent undertones vibrate as a Cadillac with a busted tail light rolls by.

Licking my lips, aware of my surroundings and the weight of conviction that won't hesitate under my buckle, I reach into my back pocket, take out my wallet, and do a quick count.

"I have three hundred bucks."

A lowrider passes in my peripheral, blaring brass-based beats and loud trumpets.

"Three fifty," I correct myself, remembering smaller bills in my pocket and feeling dark, scared-open eyes on my hands.

Stressed, restless, and wishing hard she'd just take what I fold in half and hold out to her, and run with it, I look up and past what my boy left me, over her head and toward oncoming traffic.

"What about Rhys?" she asks, still looking at me.

I swallow, watching insects circle blindly in streetlamp light.

"You wouldn't have to go home," I tell her. "You could go anywhere."

"I don't know … Can we just …" She trails off and pulls a deep breath.

"Can we wait it out?" she asks, fear still coating her voice. "I mean, what if …"

I blink, looking at the dark daycare center across the

intersection, paper bag wrapped bottles in the street, the '86 Crown Vic parked behind what's mine to deal with. I look anywhere but at her while at the end of the block, another bus turns toward us.

My pulse thumps in my palms. It throbs hard behind my eyes and fast against my ear drums. It's everywhere, stifling breathing and pushing me to do something.

"I thought you were running away," I say tightly.

"I was … "

Already too small, her voice breaks and I can't handle the sound. Sinking in my stomach hardens into an anchor between my lungs while the bus stops a block down, beeping loudly and exhaling exhaust. People get off and onto it while I weigh morals against allegiance, and both of them together against the sound I can't bear, and come up fucked no matter which way I go.

Watching the bus begin to move again, I pocket my wallet as it passes us, and I look down, meeting eyes that are helplessly desperate and waiting for mine.

"Okay," I say under a quickly-heaving heartbeat.

Visibly swallowing, she blinks, nodding and eager.

Like now, *now*—

She's ready to run.

"Let's go this way," I tell her.

As I walk, she falls in step beside me, and as we head toward the brighter lights of Rhode Island Avenue, I pull out my phone and dial the only person in D.C. I know won't ask too many questions, because if this is it, I'm taking her home.

Not to her parents.

But where I know is safest.

# a story about falling by ᔕₐᵣₐₕ

My friend's phone rings four times before she picks up.

"Hey, lion. How's it going?"

It's quiet in her background, and I hope hard she's in town.

"Esther, hey. I have a … quandary."

She chuckles. Our communication doesn't usually consist of me asking for help.

"Alright, where are you? What's up?"

Tandem steps echo in my chest, and bring the girl and I closer to a busier street. I spot a yellow and red lit Denny's down the block, and can hear commotion coming up.

"I'm on 12th NE, about to Rhode Island." Cars drive past steadily now, and I keep quiet on my right carefully in the corner of my eye. "Can you give me and a delicate situation a ride back to the harbor?"

Carefree and kind, unsuspecting and unexpecting, the club chick I only call when I'm delivering hydro asks, "How delicate?"

I glance right, bringing lamb's crown into focus. Short, black painted fingernails push back almost-black brown hair as we walk.

"You'll see."

"Sure," Esther agrees, curiosity in her voice. "Yeah. Gimme a few minutes. I'll call you when I'm close."

Rhode Island Avenue isn't shoulder to shoulder, but there are kids and people on both sides of the street, in and out of diners, drug stores and gas stations. Up on the left, *Two Girls, One Booth* is crudely well-lit and the hood around us is wide awake: derelict, dissolute, and destitute in more ways than one.

I consider waiting for Esther inside Denny's, but that would just let people better see the two of us until then, and I want out

51

of public.

I want a shower.

I want food.

I want quiet, dark-eyed and twenty-five to life out of fucking sight.

Enduring the aching fixation in my jaw, the stress stretching tighter across my shoulders, and the solidified sinking that's still pulling through me as we make our way under streetlamp light, I wish I had a hood to pull up.

I wish I had a hoodie to take off and put on my crime as we approach other pedestrians.

I remind myself that's all we are to them.

Two people, walking, minding our business just like everyone else.

But the truth twists and burns between my lungs.

I'm walking next to a missing person, and I'm the only one in the world who knows where she is.

No one pays us any real attention, but as we near a group of drunk fucks, I reach out with my right hand.

My fingertips brush soft denim, her hip, seeking a grip when smaller fingers wrap around my first two like she's assuring me.

Like I need to be reminded she's not going to run.

Like it's her I don't trust.

As we walk, side by side with her fingers around mine, I keep seeking, sliding my hand under her tee shirt until I find her belt loop. Loosing my fingers from softer ones, I curve them through her little denim noose instead.

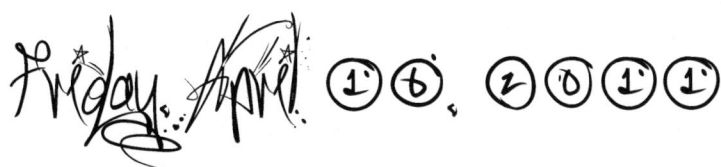

Friday, April 16, 2011

## 10:56 pm

"Well, well, well."

"Hi."

"Hello, Stems."

"Hello, Rainbow?"

"What's your name, pretty?"

Esther greets the girl in sheer black tights that I let into the front seat, and before I shut the door, the life I'm now accountable for glances up at me.

I close her into the old Volkswagen and bend to get in the back seat.

"This is Lamb," I answer, sliding to the middle and watching her look over at our pink, purple, and periwinkle haired driver. "This is Esther."

"Lamb, huh?" The friend I just made an accomplice asks, eyeing me over her shoulder as she passes her passenger freshly

Don't Let Me Go

lit bubblegum dro.

No way I'm giving her real name or anything else, I hold my hands palm up with a sealed smile.

"Alright, Stems it is," Esther replies, glancing at the kid again before starting to drive. If she notices red marks on her wrists and arms, she swallows her reaction. "What kind of music you like, sweetheart?"

"Anything." The girl in front of me shrugs. "Anything is good."

My smile loosens a little as "Love Me Do" fills the cab.

Esther's crazy in her own way, but harmless, and the '68 Type 4 is small, but we're off the street. I can keep both eyes on mixed-up innocence from here, and with every mile closer to Baltimore, stress-pressure ebbs into assuring, almost-home hope.

But I don't forget I've left the place my best friend left me.

Listening to the girls talk as the miles pass, I watch the one riding shotgun smoke and lean at ease. My narrowed-in limbs tense and I bring my hands together in my lap, popping nerve-cramped knuckles and swallowing hard.

"So you want to go to Brown?" Esther asks, exhaling a hit toward her cracked window.

"Yeah," my dark and dire strait answers, certainty and comfort in her voice now. "They have this really cool urban education policy program, for rebuilding communities and saving underprivileged schools."

"That's earnest goodness, kid."

I roll my window down.

Blocks from my house and closing in, impatience spins with second, third, and fourth thoughts. I'm starving, drained, and beyond discordant. As we turn onto Oakbridge, misgivings creep like fever-chills, slick and sick and heavy.

I want out of this car.

By the time we pull into the driveway, my vision's gone grey. My limits, the past and present, right and wrong … Everything swims in murk, but the line from where we are to my front door is clear. Concrete black and moonlit white stretch before me with the sharpest simplicity.

Esther turns in her seat, but I'm opening my door as she speaks.

"Tell Lyd I said hi."

"I will," I answer, getting out. "Thanks again."

"Thank you," Kenny tells her as I open her door.

"You're welcome. Good luck."

Esther pulls away, and boot steps echo behind mine as I walk, one hand in my hair and the other reaching for my keys. When I reach the steps, tripping the sensor, the porch light comes on, illuminating Vans I've walked whatever was sticky off of, and creating new shadows. With lamb beside me, I look both ways down my block and unlock the door.

It's darker inside than out, but the ease in pressure is undeniable.

Locking up after she enters behind me and stands to the side, I turn on track lights and head toward the kitchen. This place hasn't seen me since yesterday morning, but air conditioning just this side of cold still carries tints of fabric softener and dank pine. The sound of it quietly blowing from the vents comforts just as much as the scent, and the hesitation I felt about bringing her here lifts.

"You want some water?" I ask, opening the fridge and

grabbing a bottle.

Backlit with the low-gold glow from the living room and front silhouetted in Frigidaire brightness, pint-sized, compromised, and well-hidden under my roof nods her head.

I hand her the bottle and grab another. My stomach growls, but when I think about feeding it, my nerves disagree. I look down as she finishes a few drinks.

"Do you want something to eat?"

"No," she says gently, shaking her head, pressing together lips I can make out the shape but not the color of. "Thank you."

Starting and finishing my own bottle, I toss what's empty, point toward the stairs, and take the lead. We head to my room, and I mean to be considerate, but my own wants and needs are heavy on me too.

A shower.

Clean clothes.

My bed.

But this is still a situation.

I'm still clocked in.

Upstairs, assurance steadies and sanctions me as we get between two walls made of floor-to-ceiling windows, spilling nightlife light across all my speakers and my dresser. A subway sized print of Four Darks in Red faces the opposite wall of books and music, every bit as unorganized as always. Tendons and ligaments that haven't rested all day remain tight inside me, but my hands and shoulders loosen as I walk past unmade stars and stripes strewn across my California King.

Flipping on the bathroom light, I take a fresh towel from the cabinet and set it on the counter, pulling a deep breath before stepping back into my bedroom.

"There's a shower if you want," I tell the girl still holding a water bottle, lingering a few steps in and looking around my space.

This is where I wanted, but my chest is still sinking.

Thankful she doesn't and hasn't asked any more questions, I grab a clean tee and sweats, and set them in the bathroom, next to the towel.

"You can take the bed," I say, glancing at the faded flag, pushed around pillows and twisted sheets. "I don't—"

I reroute that train of thought.

"They're clean," I continue, picking up a pillow that's almost fallen from my bed and tossing it up with the others. Pushing my hair back from my temples, I scratch the back of my neck. "Or you can sleep on the couch if you want. Wherever you're comfortable."

"Thank you," she speaks up, drawing my attention from sun-bleached red, white, and blue to timidly low lids and vulnerable dark brown irises. "This is great. Thank you."

When she heads in and closes the bathroom door behind her, I exhale from deeper than my lungs. I chase it with another from even deeper when I hear the shower start, and I open the sliding glass door that doubles as one of the windows, and head outside.

The second-floor deck spans the entire back of the house, from my room to my sister's, down the hall. There are a few chairs and tables in the middle, and a potted clementine tree at her end. Walking down and finding a ripe one, I pluck it free and head back to my end. Leaning against the ledge, looking out at the gritty-glittering wide awake city, I roll the orange between my palms.

Exhausted, conflicted, and unable to focus on a single thought, I go back and forth between what are we going to do, and what can we do?

Dropping my eyes from vibrant skyscrapers to the fruit in my hands, I measure out a slow breath.

What can't we do?

Moscow and I both have enough funds to get away with anything, and between all four of us, we've got more than enough contacts and resources to make the darkest shit disappear.

But what D wants is Rhys.

And I don't know what's going to turn him up.

Digging carefully with my thumb, I pull the peel away and let it fall to the grass below. I've parted and eaten half the orange when a shift in the light coming through the glass behind me tugs my attention.

Turning and standing straight, I lay eyes on the one thing that might draw out and wise up this girl's reckless, forgetful, and seriously fucked brother.

With her left half glowing in soft white light, she meets my look. Black cotton swallows her like a wave, my short sleeves long on her arms and my sweatpants baggy on her legs. Her hair's piled in a bun on top of her head, showing off her neck, and when she turns off the light, there's a sensation like gripping in my gut.

Blinking to adjust to the sudden dark, I lean away from the ledge as she opens the door to come outside too. Colored incandescent by the same city nighttime as I am, she doesn't wonder or waver. Shy gratitude shines in her eyes when she glances up as she comes to stand beside me, and when I hold the orange out in offering, she nods.

I tug a cleft free, and she takes it, placing her elbows on the deck ledge and looking out. Returning my arms to the same ledge, I drag my eyes from everything that's making me conspire, and stare out toward the golden-glowing Charles Center.

But my peripheral vision stays locked.

And when small and clean and scented like me swallows softly, I break another cleft away.

I offer it without looking or speaking, and she accepts it and each piece after just the same, until my hands are empty.

# Saturday, April 17, 2011

## 7:00 am

"The number of charter schools is only growing while more and more failing schools are shut down. We're no stranger to it here in our own cities …"

Talk radio that comes on every morning as an alarm seeps into my shallow sleep.

"If the system is supposed to prepare young people for participation in the world, shouldn't we be committed to rejuvenating and supporting not just schools, but communities themselves?"

Blinking, I open tired eyes that go straight to curled up and fast asleep under the flag.

She's still in the same position she laid down in last night, on her side with both hands bent under her head on my pillow. Long brown hair remains piled on her crown, loose but neat from not stirring. For a second I wonder if she's okay, but her star-covered frame steadily rises and falls with slow sleep-breaths.

"That's why we have to take what Gonzales is doing to heart. Educators are activists, not CEOs."

Rubbing my eyes, I sit up straighter while the calm voice of morning news fills my bedroom. The girl in my bed's obviously unaffected, crashed out hard through what yesterday's adrenaline left behind, but I stand from the wingback desk chair I nodded off in and quiet the sound anyway.

On my feet, I'm every bit as heavy as I was when I finally sat down last night.

Still in yesterday's clothes—shoes, belt, fifteen hollowpoints in each mag and one in both chambers under my buckle—I didn't sleep so much as close my eyes between the sound of every car that went by, every time the air conditioning kicked on, and every internal shift of my own rhythms and uneasy readiness. Ragged between anxious and alert, I pull my phone from my pocket only to find no missed communication at all.

It's a new day, but we're still exactly where we were.

The last twenty-four hours bear down on me under fresh sunlight, and I draw dark curtains to let lamb sleep in peace as I head downstairs.

Grabbing the newspaper from the lawn, I skim headlines. I make coffee. I trade my empty cup for a toothpick, and go the basement where I water and prune prohibited plants, check trichomes, and clip what's ready. Trimming takes careful time, but two hours later, despite every attempt at seeking assuagement in normalcy, my shoulders are only heavier. My eyes burn with exhaustion, and my limbs are resistant to every movement. I want to go for a run, but I can't leave.

Overheated from the grow room and stiff with unsettlable stress, I climb the stairs back to my bedroom with the intention of changing to work out, but my space glows cool and calm, inviting rest.

The kid's still deeply asleep where I left her. She's stretched onto her back now though, and a D.A.R.E. tee shirt that's too big is twisted around her under the flag she's tangled in.

My tired and running on nearly empty pulse throbs behind my eyes as I pull them from her and head to the bathroom. With the door closed, a glance in the mirror shows me I look just like I feel: dark-circled and pale under yesterday's black. A glance at my phone reveals it's almost ten o'clock, and I still haven't heard from anyone.

For all my best friend knows, I'm still in that shithole backroom in Brookland, and it makes my blood drag like a grudge.

Tugging my shirt off, I step out of my shoes and immediately feel lighter, but even that doesn't compare to the lift that comes as I undo my belt. Pulling sixty ounces of life and death severity from my hips is simultaneously so freeing and easing, I get dizzy.

I focus on the lightness as I shower, but the cut in my brow stings under hot water, and it's hard to get out from under everything I don't know. My balance is fucked-up with unreasonable responsibility, and sooner or later, the girl I tied up, terrified and crossed state lines twice with is going to wake up.

Lingering under hot water long after I'm clean, I try to put myself in Doc Martens that echoed my footsteps, but they don't fit.

I'm not a girl.

# a story about falling by Sarah

I'm not a kid.

And I'm not innocent.

But if I was her, and someone had offered me a ticket out, I'd have taken it and never looked back.

Only, that's not true.

Because when I think along those lines, but put my sister in her brother's place—even if Lydie was beyond help—I'd ride this out for her too.

My stomach grinds around empty aching, distracting me from love so trustworthy it can't be fair. Just thinking about food comforts in a basic way. Hunger's black and white in the middle of so much grey, and I lean into it with intent.

Drying and wrapping a towel around my waist, leaving holstered protection on the counter and my clothes on the floor for new ones from my closet, I open the door to head there, but find sleepy-surprised dark eyes instead.

Sitting up in my bed, rubbing the back of her neck, morning-sunbathed and swimming in my shirt ducks her look as I balk, half-in, half-out of the bathroom.

"Sorry," she says, shifting and fidgeting while I swallow.

Glancing from her to my closet, I hold the black towel together where my guns usually are, more nervous about her seeing them than I am about being seen.

"It's okay." I pull the door closed behind me as I step out to my dresser and closet, and I feel it when she looks back up. Shy eyes are soft pressure on my bare skin, and I know she sees the scarred gunshots along the bottom of my back.

I grab the first clean clothes I touch.

Even in blinded-light, her cheeks show pink as she looks

down again when I return to the bathroom. Closing the door and clearing my head, ignoring my pulse and buttoning up with fresh black denim, I pull my belt from yesterday's jeans, loop it through today's, and holster my shit back into place.

They're no heavier in reality, but reality itself weighs twice as much now.

Pulling an old black V-neck over my head and a breath to balance myself, I step back into my room.

"Are you hungry?" I ask, tossing laundry away.

She nods when I glance over.

"Do you ..." She has a closed hand over her mouth and sincerity in her eyes.

Shaking out my damp hair and finger-combing it back, I stand and wait in the middle of my room.

"This is a really weird question," she warns lightly.

In the midst of everything we're in, I can't help laughing a little. I smile, and weight all over and inside me sways.

"Okay," I say so she'll continue. "Ask me a really weird question."

Behind busted little knuckles, the corners of her smile peek through while she contemplates. It reminds me of how relaxed she was yesterday between Easy-E and Elvis Presley, only there's no opposing effects.

Just a feeling like leaning.

"I really want to brush my teeth," she finally confesses. "But like ... I mean ... Toothbrush?"

It's mostly an exhale, but I laugh more this time.

Sharing my toothbrush feels like the most inculpable thing I've done in as long as I can remember.

## a story about falling by Sarah

"Yeah." I nod, heading to the bathroom once more and flipping on the light as she stands up from stars and stripes. "Come here."

## 11:07 am

"od cured me. You gotta believe."

"I have to eat or I can't take my pill."

"Decaf, sweetheart."

"Order up!"

"You know why blondes are more fun?"

"Hi, welcome to Rita's!"

Amidst a crowd of mostly older truck drivers, the sandy-haired woman behind the counter calls out to people who enter behind the kid and I, while we face the chalkboard menu. Late morning sunshine pours into the corner cafe that smells like coffee and pancake batter while ever-quiet on my right surveys the crowd. Still in my clothes, plus my hoodie, she tucks sleep-wavy hair behind both ears and presses the backs of sleeve-covered fingers to her lips like she's unsure.

When she looks up, I meet light-reflecting dark eyes, and

when she doesn't move her fingers or say anything, I bend my knees and lean down.

"You okay?" I ask under the commotion.

"It's really crowded," she answers, the faint hint of my Crest on her breath as she drops her hand to hoodie pockets.

It is, but unlike the busy bars and streets of D.C. last night, the heart of the harbor is safe because it's home to me. I know there's no one here that recognizes this person, and further, nobody here has anything to say to BPD.

"It's okay." I nod as she looks up again, nodding too.

Hunger that's two days old and has taken the place of anxiety scrapes through me as full plates hit the counter and the waitress looks to us, next in line.

"Do you know what you want?" I ask before stepping forward.

"Um, no. Go ahead," she says. "I'll decide while you order."

"What can I get for you guys?"

"Can we get two bacon, egg and cheese everything bagels with double bacon, a side of home fries, a ham and swiss on whole wheat, gravy, and … A cinnamon roll."

While the waitress writes it all down and rings me up, I grab a toothpick from the counter dispenser and glance at the girl next to me. Biting it between my back teeth, I watch dainty brown brows dig together over the beginning of her smile.

"Is that for us?"

I finish the curve her lips started on my own.

"No." I shake my head, too hungry to be sheepish. "That's for me."

She laughs a little as I extend my hand in offering, and she steps forward.

"Can I get a sausage, egg and cheese bagel, plain?"

"Yep, anything else?"

"Um." She rocks from her heavy heels to her tip-toes, but doesn't look at me. "Can I have double bacon on mine, too?"

My grin only grows.

"Of course," the waitress says. "Is that it for you guys?"

I glance downright.

"Do you want coffee?" I ask.

"Coke?" She asks back, looking from me to the the waitress. "Can you guys make vanilla Cokes?"

Bleach-blonde and tired-eyed behind the counter nods, and I hold up my fingers to make that two. When she asks, "To go?" I nod.

They give us the food in brown paper bags that grease shows through, in the cut-off bottom of a box. I carry it out while good in my hoodie grabs white Styrofoam cups I know are filled with old fashioned crushed ice and real vanilla. Letting her in the front of my Buick, I set the food in the back and when I come around to the driver's side, she's already unlocked it.

Quiet but easy inside the '65 Riviera, I turn from Light Street onto Lombard, avoiding turns we didn't take yesterday. Nearly-noon sun that wasn't in my eyes on the way here shines in, and I grab my shades from the visor while the girl in shotgun passes me one of the Cokes.

Lifting the lid, I drive with my left hand and sip with my right, and it hits my lips like summertime. All the carefreedom, old school irresponsibilities and small crimes of being seventeen flow with each drink, and next to me, the kid turns on the radio. Twisting the dial between static, talk, and pop, she finally settles

## a story about falling by Sarah.

on a beat I knew years before her. East Coast roots, dapper rhythm and a cocky tempo surround us, and I lean a little, sipping from my cup to curb my smile.

Lamb turns it up.

## 12:08 pm

"On their way to their fourteenth consecutive losing season in a row."

"This recipe can be a base for any of your favorite—"

"... triple homicide in their home. Police say—"

"Do you have a structured settlement?"

"How long? How long have you known you loved me?"

"I'm sorry, Corporal Capeman. Inspector Gadget always works alone."

The girl sitting on my living room floor kicks her untied boots off and flips channels while I set the box on the coffee table and sit on the carpet too, slouching back against the couch to accommodate solid weight under my buckle. Grabbing the corner of the box, I pull it toward myself the same time she reaches into it for the bags.

# a story about falling by Sarah

She laughs lightly, and all my tense muscles yearn to loosen.

Scooting back to slouch too, she criss-crosses her legs and thanks me as I pass her the biggest of three bagels.

Save for the cartoons she stopped on, we're silent while food fills, and it eases everything. My sense of balance steadies as I eat, and muscles that want to relax, finally do. Even as I start to feel full, I take another bite just because it's good, and pieces of egg and bacon fall onto the the foil wrapping in my lap, making downplayed and implicated giggle a little.

She takes as long to finish her single bagel as I do to consume my small feast, but I can't finish all I ordered. Halfway through the home fries and two layers into the cinnamon roll, I set it down and lean further, away from the couch and all the way down onto my back. Sated and stretched comfortably out on thick carpet, the weight on my hips is the only heaviness I feel.

Crumpling trash and extending her legs, the kid hums as she finishes, and climbs up onto the couch. I turn my head without thinking and when I see her sinking into overstuffed cushions, pulling my hood up over her head and my sleeves down around her hands as she lies down, she smiles.

"That was so good," she says. "Thank you."

Bending my right arm behind my head, I lay my left over my so-content stomach.

"You're welcome."

Laid-back minutes drift, and when Inspector Gadget credits roll, I sit up, taking another drink of vanilla Coke and opening the side table drawer to further gratify satisfaction. Pulling out a tray, ZigZags, and a small jar of Skywalker OG, I move to the unoccupied end of the couch.

71

"Can I?" sleepy-sounding but not sleeping asks, pulling my attention, watching me without lifting her head. "Can I roll it?"

I pass her the tray and she sits up.

Pristine as can be rolls a professional level joint.

"Just half a little baby roach, huh?" I ask, echoing her defensive words from almost twenty-four hours ago before lighting up.

She shrugs, her smile a small confession to maybe a little more than she lets on as I fill my chest.

Between deep breaths and lazy limbs, calm nerves and a hazy head, I check my phone for the time. Noon burns slowly into afternoon without a word from anyone, and smoke and steady stillness eventually have my train of thought wandering.

Long after the joint's out, the girl at the other end of my couch keeps touching her hair. Brushing the back of her head like just the contact feels good, her fingertips linger there.

Not messing up her sleep-bun or taking it down.

Just touching.

Slow and subtle as my pulse.

Until she slides her hand higher, undoing whatever's holding her hair in place. She shakes it all gently out, and soft provocation glides clear through me.

The tugging I've felt since she stepped into the light last night takes easily over as this lamb in my clothes uses all her fingers to comb through dark brown waves, sending my own scent into the air between us. Black walnut, clean cotton, and fresh: it's me but it's her, and my fleeting eyes don't think about not looking.

She doesn't see me, but the sight of her hair still damp at the ends makes thoughts I've shut down on principle alone earnestly unavoidable.

# a story about falling by Sarah

Rhys is this girl's brother.

Moscow is my best friend.

I'm the guy.

I drive.

I bury.

I deliver.

I do everything that needs doing, but I'm a guy too, and there's a girl next to me in nothing but my tee-shirt and sweats. On a purely intrinsic level, I know it's more than just her hair that smells like me right now. Bending my knee and keeping my eyes straight, I ignore knowing her skin holds my scent too, but every shake of her hands through her hair heightens awareness and deepens basic concentration.

My jaw tenses, and my teeth need, and I think about bringing one of her palms up to my mouth, just to ease the ache for something, anything to sink into.

I rub my eyes.

Trees have me daydreaming, and I know I'm going too far in my mind.

I'm not going to do it, but imagining her palm under my lips, I can't help thinking about bringing her other palm to my dick.

My chest throbs silently between smoke-pressure and thoughts that have slipped out of control. It's work to keep my breathing normal and harder work to not wonder what crucial without meaning to be would feel like underneath me.

Right here.

On her back, on this couch.

With my shirt pushed up and off her, and sunlight shining in on exposed skin.

I drag my hand down my face and reach for the roach. Smoke fills my lungs as I light it and pass it to her, but uninhibited curiosity remains rooted in the space between them.

I can't help wondering what she sounds like when she's close, if she's ever even gone that far. Her eyes gleam with a wholesomeness that's missing from everyone else I know, an unfucked-up capacity to love with hope instead of expectation, even when someone she loves has become the shadiest deadbeat we all know.

Leaving the clip with undone and too delicate for her own good or mine, I stand up and head to the bathroom.

Cool water clears my head, but when my body doesn't back down after a few splashes, I focus on my cut in the mirror and clean it carefully. Remembering how I got it more than does the trick, and by the time I've got a butterfly bandage over where lamb split me, pressure and urgency have left my dick and settled in the base of my spine, forcing me upright.

But *we're doing this and that's it* feels like too late, and forever ago now.

Pulling my phone from my back pocket, I call Sonny as I head to my room. Ignoring stars and stripes that are just how she left them, I pocket a few Jolly Ranchers from my dresser, opening one and pressing it to the roof of my mouth. With the phone between my ear and my shoulder, I grab the laundry basket that holds more than just my own clothes now and keep slowly dissolving candy in place with my tongue.

I hang up when Sonny's voicemail answers on my way to the laundry room where I toss everything in to wash together, and lean against the machine after starting it. Sunlight creeps in from

74

the little window that faces the driveway as I scroll to Moscow's name in my phone, but keep going, down to Rhys'.

Unsteady between considering and knowing better, I'm caught off guard by a car pulling up, and the second I recognize the front end, my heart drops to the floor.

I love Lyd with all that I am.

This is her home too.

But I didn't think she'd come home for spring break.

And then it hits me.

She probably thought I wouldn't be here either.

I move quickly, but her key's in the door and she's got it open by the time I'm back upstairs. Her girlfriend and four other chicks are with her, and my stomach falls when they look from me to my guest on the couch, looking back at them with confused eyes and my half-eaten cinnamon roll in her hand.

The simple sight heats my heart, but doesn't change reticent beats.

"Hey," Lydie says, smiling but surprised as she glances from me, to a girl she's never seen, and back to me. She shakes her head, but it's just to get hair as dark and only slightly longer than mine out of her eyes.

"I thought you guys were going to the Cherry Blossom thing. I didn't know … We can go, dude. I'm sorry."

"No, come on." I shake my head too, waving my sister and all of them in like I didn't just make her, the one she loves, and her four friends all accessories in serious shit.

I have, but no threat's getting in here, and I'm not turning her away from a place that's her safe space too.

Our parents do enough of that.

"So …" Hanging in the entryway as I close the door, the only person I share blood and a name with that isn't toxic starts like she's going to ask why I'm here instead of in D.C., but Lyd's smart. There's a girl in my clothes and smoke in our living room. I let her think what she wants. I wouldn't lie if she asked, one on one, what's really going on, but she's not going to. My only family for all intents and purposes isn't in the dark, but she's not nosy.

She's been through shit of her own, and knows enough about me and my friends.

"So," her girlfriend, Denise, echoes, all long red curls and a smile like fuck anything that's awkward. Reaching into her bag, she pulls out two good to go cigarillos. "Blunts?"

Another girl behind her holds up a bottle of Firefly. "Shots?"

As we move into the living room, the box breakfast came in, brown bags and familiar Styrofoam cups become instant common ground.

"You guys went to Rita's?" Lyd asks. Glancing between me and quiet on my right, eyes the same hazel-blue flecked as mine beam with memories of our own and glint the little bit of triumph that comes with putting pieces together.

"Amazing, right?" she continues.

Next to me, with her legs bent under herself and her knee pressed against the side of my thigh, my federal offense with a beating heart nods.

"Life changing," she agrees with a grin.

"CL must think you're pretty cool."

I shortstop her, "Lyd—"

"Come on, I'm just teasing. I'm Lydie," she says, playfully-natured and extending her hand in greeting.

# a story about falling by Sarah

Close enough that my personal space is ours, only getting warmer, understated but upbeat and mine to keep an eye on shakes my sister's hand.

"Lamb," she says.

I smile.

It's easier than it should be: slighting the facts, sitting next to this person I've known for years but never really knew, and leaning into her laugh. I'm comfortable as we light and drink and pass with the television still on but the sound off. Afternoon sun burns more orange than yellow through the windows, turning toward setting while Lyd and her girl bring up the dinner and party plans they had before they knew I was here.

"We were going to cook out back and call some people. Nothing big," two years younger and twice as smart as me says. "Just, you know, maybe turn it up a little ..."

Liability that smells like me exhales a little white cloud in my peripheral. Her smaller fingertips touch my own as she passes the dutch, and the impulse to bring her hand up to my lips with it flickers through me.

"That sounds so good," she says.

Her voice is low and lush and lazy, slow smoke and thick, crushed velvet, and I like how indulgent, and supple-undone it sounds. I like how relaxed she is and that she could eat again, and as she pushes her fingers through long, bourbon and coffee colored waves, my high-attention is fucked, singular, and all hers.

Again.

I shift my position, and two guns weigh on me.

"Just a few people," I tell Lydie, reality fraying the edges of my ease. "Just your close friends."

77

## 10:36 pm

"I don't wanna fuck you. You can't even sing."

"Turn it up!"

"You had to sing or something to get some pussy."

"What do you know about ODB?"

"Man, come on. Turn it up!"

"Were these kids even alive when this song came out?"

Next to me in a chair on the grass, facing the same boys and girls who aren't actually that much younger than us, Sonny shakes his head.

Lamping under the stars while gritty, headnodic beats flow with the nighttime breeze, I sip Sailor from a glass. Patio light and downtown Baltimore's glow illuminate the twenty or so people dancing on the other side of the pool. I was hesitant about having a crowd in my backyard, but my only reason to be sways easily and smiles brightly across from me, like this is exactly what she

78

ran away for.

I'd be lying if I said I didn't like it.

As she heads inside with Lyd and an empty cup, I turn to my boy, whose girl is next to him.

He hasn't seen or heard from Moscow either, not since Violet showed up in D.C. last night.

No news is good news, right?

I take another drink.

More people show as the night rolls on. Mostly Lyd's friends, but a few of mine too, thanks to Sonny. Solo and Banks, Mal and the boys, Ev and his girl, and an already open bottle of red wine, all meet my charge.

But just like with Esther, and Lyd, she's Lamb to all of them.

And she fits right in with my sweats rolled down and my shirt knotted up, barely baring the bottom of her belly and the tops of her hips while she follows rhythm with her whole body.

Under the music, Sonny says something else, but I can't concentrate, because across the yard and lined in city nightlights, this girl steals glances under her lashes. She knows I'm looking. She's letting me see, but it's affecting me on levels I don't think she realizes.

Sonny's talking, but the music, him, and reality hanging in wait are all just background.

Lamb's bottom lip and low-lidded look are all that's clear in this haze.

Dipping with a drop in the beat, all that's in focus for me pushes her hair back, holding it up off her neck with one hand. She tilts her head, lost in the hook and riding it with eyes closed like she's made of music. Like music's her lover, moving inside her.

My heart beats and my head spins, and I shift in my seat because I feel it.

My whole body knows this song.

Next to me, Sonny laughs. I look over, and he shakes his head like he saw what I saw. Like he saw me see it.

"Aww," he kids, meeting my eyes, "What, are you soft on her?"

Nothing about any of this feels soft.

Still shaking his head, he laughs some more, but lower now. "That's fucked-up, man."

Instinct and protection-heavy hips all but ache.

"Yeah," I agree, taking another drink.

Lighthearted commotion on the other side of the pool reclaims my attention, and my pulse knots tightly when I look over and don't see her for a beat.

But then she's there.

Here.

On her way to where I am.

"I'm sorry," she says, but she's beaming, inspecting the alcohol-soaked left side of my D.A.R.E. shirt and holding out an empty cup. "It wasn't me."

Tugging out black cotton that's sticking to her, making it drip, she laughs.

I smile, and it feels good from the inside all the way out. I nod toward the house.

"Come on."

My place is dimly lit, completely still, and muffled quiet as I close the patio door behind us. A little intoxicated and entirely

80

too alluring takes straight to the stairs, and I swallow as I follow close behind.

Climbing carefully, she pulls all her hair over her right shoulder ,and the bare bend of her neck glimmers under low track lights. My bearings swim and I lick my lips, near enough that all I smell is vanilla, rum, and girl.

"I think Denise bumped into Carissa, who bumped into me," she says, the buoyancy I can't see audible in her tone. "Or maybe it was Erica. I'm not sure."

As we reach the top of the stairs, she glances over her shoulder, seeking my eyes with her lip between her teeth, and I wonder if it's intentional.

The looks.

Her lip.

How she keeps touching her hair.

"It's okay," I say, meeting her eyes.

Illuminated with the harbor's night-brightness, my room's better lit than the rest of the house. I head to my closet as we enter, and while I flip through hangers, her bare feet pad across the carpet, stopping over by my speakers. Grabbing the next shirt I touch, a plain black V-neck, I turn to face her.

"Can the records play through these too?" she asks, gesturing from a shelf of vinyl to the surrounding system.

Stepping forward, I nod. "Yeah."

"Does it sound a lot different? Like than a CD?"

I hand her the shirt.

"It does."

"Thanks," she says, alone and glowing with me under the neon skyline. It glints in her eyes as she looks up before turning

81

around and setting every uncertainty I had totally straight.

Tugging damp black cotton over her head, lamb exposes her whole back.

Vanilla-bean brown hair falls soft like down over naked skin and there are two little dimples at the base of her spine that the gritty shine of Baltimore nightlife can't reach. She's all graceful shoulder blades and subtle curves as she lifts her arms to pull on the new shirt, and I've never felt captivated by or so attracted to someone's back before.

Pressing down on my body's immediate reaction for half a second, I turn as she does, and bring my hand to the back of my head.

"So," she says, leaving the first shirt draped over my desk chair. "Do you own anything not black?"

I laugh, and spiced rum swims through me, making this feel easy.

Or maybe it's her.

"No," I return, grinning sarcastically. "I wear black on the outside because black is how I feel inside."

Safe in my space and cute in my clothes really laughs, and I want to go down in it. All the way. I want swallowed up and always surrounded in how she sounds right now.

"Okay," she continues, composing herself and keeping my eyes until she steps past me. "Where'd you get the flag?"

The corners of my lips waver, but I stay with her.

"It used to fly off Domino Sugars," I answer. "Remember?"

Approaching my bed, she nods as she sits down by pillows and runs her hand over old stars.

"My dad worked there," I say, toeing the frayed end of

weathered red hanging from the corner of my bed with my shoe. She's still smiling, so I don't tell her about layoffs or food stamps or fights that never ended, or that I've only kept the flag he stole solely because I like how it feels: heavily-threaded, wind-whipped, and faded-perfect soft.

"What does CL stand for?"

She looks at me with sincerity and hope as she leans back, and my heart thumps steadily between my lungs.

I'd tell her anything now.

"You writing a book?" I ask in turn, brows raised in teasing.

Dark eyes shine bright. "Maybe."

I sit down at the foot of my bed, reclining back against the same wall as her and popping my knuckles as I rest my hands in my lap.

"We had to perform *The Wizard of Oz* in third grade."

My hands aren't what I care to look at.

"Everybody had a part. Dorothy. The witch. Toto. The flying monkeys, everybody."

Turning my head, I give my eyes what they want.

Pink cheeked from drinking, relaxed back like she's at home in my space, lamb's waiting for my attention when I finally lay my look on her.

"Who were you?" she asks.

Not rolling my eyes, only because I can't take them off her, I lick my lips again.

"The Cowardly Lion."

A giggle comes out through her nose, and she brings her hand up to cover it.

"Yeah." I smile. "Sonny thought that was pretty funny too."

She takes her hand down, letting me see her mouth as she asks, "Who was he?"

"The Tin Man."

Totally tenderly, this girl takes hold of all that I am with just her eyes. Gathering and pulling fills my chest, and my throat feels full too.

We're not touching, but she's got me.

"All heart," she says.

I look deeper.

"All along."

# Saturday, April 17, 2011

## 7:00 am

"Repaving will continue on I-95 southbound, keeping it down to two lanes through the next week. Lots of traffic again this morning with the Orioles at home and folks returning from the annual Cherry Blossom Festival ..."

Morning radio pulls me from rest, and I blink hard, squinting against sunlight flooding through open curtains.

"Expect a high of seventy-four today, partly cloudy, lows in the mid-sixties this evening. No rain in sight until maybe Tuesday ..."

Rubbing my eyes, I stretch my legs from the sitting position I nodded off in at the end of my bed and look to my right to find lamb, curled on her side. Wrapped in my black, with a new day lighting all her peaceful features, she's still on top of the flag, sleeping soundly.

"Howard County police are still investigating a shooting

85

from Friday night that left two injured and one dead, and are offering up to $2,500 for information leading to an arrest ..."

Standing, I shut off the news and turn back to my bed.

The missing girl that's still mine to look out for breathes evenly, and I remember her dreamy-dark eyes slipping closed last night. I kept talking until intermittent little hums faded into steadily silent in and exhales, and as the party wound down outside, I stayed awake right where I was for hours.

First with my head back against the wall, staring up at my ceiling.

Then out the window.

Then with my hand over closed eyes.

Because how did things get so fucked?

I'd do for Lyd whatever I could, anything—just like Kenny is for Rhys—but Lyd isn't my brother.

Moscow is.

And regret at not having stayed put burdened me while my call to loyalty curled up and found comfort in my bed.

Dragging my hand down my face, I head to my closet.

I've made Lydie and her girlfriend, my friends, all those kids into witnesses and accomplices. I've further implicated Sonny and I left him last night just so I could sit by a girl, who underneath all of this is a person I abducted, bound, unbound, and have kept in my house, off the radar for more than twenty-four hours now.

I grab clean clothes and trudge to the bathroom in shoes I slept in.

Again.

The two 9x19s under my belt impart their weight and

influence into every step, but as I close the door behind me, they're nothing compared to the burden in the bottom of my chest.

The lightness that unsteadies me as I disarm, and take my Vans and everything else off to shower is more intense today than yesterday. I don't linger under the water this morning. I make myself clean and my focus clear, and I buckle back up under fresh black jeans.

The pressure in my ribcage pounds as I pocket a phone with still no missed calls or texts, and I think again about cutting out the middle man altogether.

I could call Rhys myself.

I could handle all of this, myself.

Swallowing with effort that strains, I grab the clean white tee off the counter. It's in my left hand as I open the door to let out some steam, and find that my transgression's slipped underneath Old Glory while I've been away from her.

Curled on her opposite side now, facing away from dawn's too-brightness, only the top of lamb's crown peeks out and the slope from her shoulder, to her waist, to her hip is a line I'm suddenly dying to know by heart.

Just like that, fast asleep in the sunshine under stars that are mine, this runaway clears every conviction I thought I was made of into a body of entirely blank slates.

I pull my shirt on as I walk around my bed to the side she's facing, and bend at my knees. Crouched down, I bring my fingers to hers, curved over her chin.

"Hey." I keep my voice low as I tap the top of her hand, swallowing the prolonged impulse to kiss the red marks on her wrist.

For as heavy a sleeper as I thought she was with the radio making no difference these last two mornings, she pulls a deep breath through her nose and wakes easily. I drop my hand when she rubs her lids and stretches out under red, white, and blue, not lifting her head as she blinks, and brings me into focus.

"Hey," she says quietly.

Her smile just barely begins, and just-woke-up eyes emanate vulnerability so open, so trusting, the solidified pressure between my lungs throbs. It hurts, but in this sweet, inviting sort of way that I want to give in to.

"Hey," I say again, holding those eyes.

Silhouetted in soft dawn, she glows.

"Hey," she repeats, nestling between my pillows and sheets, resting her cheek on her hands.

I feel my grin grow as I speak.

"You want some breakfast?"

She nods, and hair that's sleep-tangled falls across her face.

"Can I take you somewhere?" she asks, brushing it away. "It's safe."

Lightheaded between blank slates and the wholehearted way this person looks at me, I nod.

"Yeah."

I wait downstairs with armed hips and eager feet, leaning against the back of the couch with my keys in my hand, my phone in my pocket, and some unsteadiness in my frame. My train of thought wanders while my stomach twists and pangs, and I tell myself food will help.

Outside, I let lamb into the Buick and as I get in, close the door and turn the key, instinct crashes over me like a tidal wave.

Go.

Just go.

Drive.

"It's so bright," my passenger says with a small yawn, pulling my attention from a current of severe insistence. Sunlight splashes through neighborhood trees, making her squint and turn to me.

I pass her my shades from the visor.

With my hood draped over her hair and my old-school Saratogas covering her eyes, little perilous looks crazy precious, and when she smiles high, warmth unfolds all through me.

"Which way?" I ask.

"Left." She points. "It's just outside of town."

I pull onto the street, and she guides the way while I drive.

It takes around half an hour to get there, but when she points out our destination, I chuckle from sentimentally deep in my heart.

Turning toward the row of shops on Loch Raven Boulevard, I check out the blue and white building that's more of a stand tucked between Joey's Pawn and Gun, and a Sunoco gas station.

"Snow cones don't really count as breakfast, you know," I say as I park and turn in my seat to give her completely to my eyes.

Moving her hand under my hood and through her hair, she shrugs playfully.

"They do when you're eighteen."

The relief from my marrow to my shoulders is monumental feeling, and my chuckle dissolves into a full laugh.

I grab my keys as she watches me through my own lenses and tugs my hood back up over her ponytail. She keeps them both on as we head inside Lush Crush.

Pop music plays from somewhere in the background and a surly-about-being-up-early-during-spring-break girl sits behind the counter. Two more hang out near the register, keeping her company.

"Hey," the cashier morosely intones. "Do you guys know what you want?"

Unruffled, lamb steps forward to look at the flavor board while I hang back. The small shop smells like strawberry and coconut, and the air conditioning unit taking up the only window blows less than quietly.

I smile.

Up less than an hour but full of waking life, eighteen and equilibrium-shaking shuffles on her feet in front of me, rolling from their outsides to their insteps. Crossing one Doc Martened ankle over the other and then the other way around, she tilts her hooded head like she can't decide and like dancing about it might somehow help.

Running my right hand over the start of stubble on my chin, I step forward.

"What are you getting?" she asks, taking my sunglasses off and tucking them into the collar of my hoodie.

I glance at the board and read the first flavor I see before returning my eyes to her.

"Wedding cake."

I snort before I even get the words all the way out, and she giggles so hard she brings her hand up and ducks her head.

"Come on," I encourage, nudging her elbow with mine while laughter hangs on the edge of my voice. "What do you want?"

# a story about falling by Sarah

"I don't know." She rocks on her feet, glancing from me to the board, and back again. "Honeydew melon? Tutti frutti?" She laughs. "Why is Buzz Lightyear a flavor?"

Half in agreement and half at the levity of being here, I laugh harder, feeling it all the way in my stomach.

Doe-eyed and drawing me with simple proximity looks back to the list and bends her fingers together in front of her lips, fidgeting.

"Wedding cake actually sounds really good," she says.

"It is," the cashier interjects, coarsely-voiced and impatient-eyed, like it's our fault she has to be here today.

Lamb shifts her weight to her left foot, bringing herself that much closer to my side. Hiding a little, biting her smile, she pockets her hands before looking up.

"Is that really what you're getting?"

"Yeah." I nod, still grinning, careless about anything but the curve of her lips. "Here."

Hovering my hand over the small of her back, I bring her with me as I stride forward.

"One giant wedding cake and one ..." I look around the board. "What do you call it when you mix two flavors?"

Stuck at work is unimpressed.

"A bikini," she says.

Light as a feather as I reach for my wallet, I return my eyes to shy on my right. "Alright, so, one giant wedding cake and one ..."

I slow down and say it extra seriously, "Tutti frutti ... Wedding cake ... Bikini."

Lamb laughs again, and it rings around my heartbeat.

The cashier makes our ices while her friends roll their eyes toward their phones. I pay, and the girl who makes it hard for me to see anything else grabs our cups. She walks in front of me but turns, opening the door with her back.

"Have you ever had one of these?"

Outside is busier than it was just a few minutes ago. The sun's brighter. Birds dip and sing. Cars and buses roll by.

"A snow cone?" I ask, walking toward her as she continues walking backwards, facing me.

A hundred shades of orange and pink behind her, morning comes through between skyscrapers, backlighting her and giving all my black a golden lining.

"Well, yeah, but from here," she clarifies, ambling carefully while I commit this moment to permanent memory.

This is what I want to stay with me.

However everything plays out, this is what I want for life.

Not muffled screams.

Not terrified eyes.

This.

And I'm not ready to take another step forward.

Not yet.

So, I stop.

And she stops, too.

And we're paused in the middle of this dirty little parking lot, and I don't know what comes next or how badly I've maybe fucked up, but as I stand still, my most complicated risk comes closer. She stands directly in front of me, and I'm simultaneously exhilarated and made meek, humbled by headstrong trust and reckless courage at five foot two and smiling.

Wanting to see her, I reach out and push my hood back, off

her head. Dark brown hair shines almost red in the sunlight, and her eyes glimmer brightly as I lift my sunglasses to her crown.

"Not since I was a kid," I answer, unsteady on my feet but so awed.

"When I was little," she starts, at ease and still holding both cups as the city wakes up around us. "They'd put frozen custard in the bottom sometimes. So you could get like, peach or cherry or banana or whatever, and then have vanilla goodness to mix in halfway through."

Listening to her talk, I feel unburdened from gravity, like I'm not standing on the ground so much as skimming along the surface of something new.

"My mom used to take us out as a reward for good report cards. We'd have pizza at the mall over there, and then come here for dessert."

The corners of her eyes tighten, and the curve of her lips wavers.

"Rhys kind of ruined that, I guess," she says lowly.

Grief stings with resentment, while behind her, down the block, a white and blue Caprice turns onto the street, and everything in and around me boils down.

My whole life, there's nothing I've dealt or spilled or buried that's as anywhere near as illicit or detrimental as what's in front of me right now.

All this girl wants to do is protect her brother and be a teacher she never had.

Lamb's everything innocent.

But she's a life sentence.

And as the cop cruises slowly closer, I don't blink as I reach out again.

I rest my hands on little hips like they belong there, because whatever happens, this is my fall.

Not my brother's.

Not hers.

Mine.

Fiercely on fire between tall buildings, the sun burns blindingly bright while mine to catch leans sweetly into my palms, and BPD rolls past.

## 10:22 am

"Remember, never tell anyone you're home alone and never give anyone your address."

"I'll say Mom can't come to the phone."

"Smart thinking."

"Now I know."

"And knowing is half the battle."

As G.I. Joe ends, the girl still wearing my hoodie sits up. Across from me on the couch, she rolls her neck and touches the back of her hair. Still hungry, I slouch further into the cushions and rest my hands on my stomach. She yawns, and I look over, watching as she stretches out her arms and sits up straighter.

"Do you want to eat?" I ask.

Another yawn pulls slowly through her, and she nods.

"Yeah. I want a shower first though."

Upstairs, I grab fresh sweats and a new tee, and give her

Don't Let Me Go

privacy.

We've been mostly quiet since we got back, but downstairs, it's much louder without her. From the flow of central air conditioning and the hum of the fridge, to the birds and cars outside, I'm aware of every sound. I tie up the trash and take it out, and when I come back in, I can hear the shower running one floor up.

With Lyd and Denise still sleeping, I clean a little more in the kitchen, eat a few handfuls of Cheerios from the box, and settle back down on the couch. I order two pizzas and the cashier on the other end of the phone tells me it will probably take over an hour.

"We're a driver short today. Sorry."

"That's okay," I say, drinking what's left of melted vanilla-cake cream-ice.

"Alright, so one smoky barbecue chicken with bacon and one Italian Trio. Anything else?"

I glance at lamb's boots under the corner table.

"Double bacon," I add.

"Okay, um, the Italian comes with pancetta and prosciutto."

Leaning my head back, I close my eyes and listen to shower water run.

"I know."

Checking the time as I hang up, there are two texts from Sonny but nothing else.

*Went to Denny's after the party and Carissa felt bad about spilling her drink on Lamb. So she drew her a card on a napkin.*

*Then threw up on it.*

Laughing, I re-pocket my phone and reach for my tray. I roll

96

# a story about falling by Sarah

two joints before just out of the shower steps down the stairs in new black and grey cotton. Barefoot and bright-eyed, grenadine-cheeked from the hot water, she gathers her damp hair over one shoulder and works her fingers through it. As she takes her spot on my couch, notes of warm cedar and wet cognac—my own soap—mixed with that soft, almost powdery scent that is all, only and naturally *girl*, float toward me. Surrounding my senses and settling between my hips, fresh nearness creates pressure and the need for pressure as she shakes out wavy-wet dark brown.

"I seriously feel a thousand times better," she says. "Thank you."

Instinct and wonder push into my pulse as she rests her arm on the back of the couch and her head in her hand, and brings her eyes to mine. Nodding, I light one of the joints, and she scoots a little closer.

As we pass it back and forth, I tell her about Carissa's card, and she giggles with her hand over her mouth.

She tells me the first time she got high she forgot how to blink, and when I say I'm glad she remembered, she smiles so wide her eyes close tightly.

"Come on, hey, open up," I tell her around a hit. "Now's a terrible time to forget again."

Adorable in the clouds brings her hand up to cover a grin that won't quit, and smoked-low lids lift over high-raised cheeks. Lashes that can't be, but still look damp, bat slowly over dreamy-dark eyes like she's showing me she remembers.

And this girl …

She's just showing me her eyes.

But it's the sexiest thing I've ever seen.

Her laugh melts into a hum, and her hand falls.

"Did you suddenly forget how, too?"

Caught in my awe, I close my own eyes and laugh at myself.

By the end of the joint, we're slouched-euphoric into the cushions. Lazily dug-in, there's space between us, but even as our heads rest against the back of the couch, uninhibited eye contact holds, curious and timid-insistent. We're trading stories and comparing shared memories, and when I lean up to set down what's left, she asks if I remember snapbacks and cargo shorts.

"Of course." I settle back against micro-suede cushions and find my place in her eyes.

"Did you forget about Bubble Tape and The Backstreet Boys?"

Her smile heartens all of me, and I'm doing it again, engraving this moment into myself for keeps.

"Every girl goes through the boy band phase, okay?"

"Yeah? Does every girl go through the shoes-that-turn-into-roller-skates phase, too?"

"Hey," she mock defends. "My Heelys were tight."

Cracking up because she just said tight, I stretch out my legs and drape my arm over my empty stomach. Hungry and wondering how long it's been since I ordered food, I check my phone to find nothing from no one, and that it actually hasn't been that long at all.

Unbending her legs too, so within my reach lies back a little, stretching over the side of the sofa, making a shape that begs to be traced.

As she sits back up, moving her fingers through still not quite dry hair, it puts the scent of me-on-her back in the air between us. I swallow, but it stops, stuck at the bottom of my throat, and I bring my hand up, pressing and rubbing over my sternum.

"You okay?" she asks.

I look over, but the sound of a car outside steals all that I am.

I'm up before she can blink, and my everywhere-beating heart races as the Impala pulls in next to Lyd's Jetta. I watch through the translucent curtains as Moscow and Bax get out, and at the sound of their doors closing, endangered and endeared to me more than she knows speaks up in the smallest voice.

"What is it?"

I force a steadying breath, and my whole body braces beneath the surface. Under adrenaline, truth runs clear.

Fight or flight shouldn't be a reaction to your friends.

"It's okay," I say calmly, giving her my eyes. "Stay right there. It's okay."

Trustful dark browns sink in fear, but she nods, and I center myself.

Strolling carelessly with his eyes hidden behind mirrored aviators when I open my door, my boy smiles so high, his dimples show. I stand aside to let him in, and he drops a low-five handshake.

"Morning, sunshine," he greets.

Under his own sunglasses, Baxter follows with a lesser grin, and I glance up and down my block before closing the door. I'm hit with the faintest scent of wet metal underneath leftover smoke, and the influx of lamb's fear into my living room takes me straight back to a black light.

My veins crawl.

In the corner of my eye, she's right where she should be,

sitting razor straight and facing this way.

I don't have to look to know it.

But my friends do.

"How was D.C.?" I ask flatly, bringing their focus back to me.

Dolzhikov pushes dark frames up into clean blonde hair, and his pupils are wide, but not blown.

"Can I talk to you?" Stoned, he glances from me to the banister.

I shift my eyes from him to Bax while panic engulfs everything from my inner ear to my lungs from almost ten feet away.

Facing my closest friend, I look over his short shoulder and give the kid on my couch my eyes.

"Yeah," I say.

Totally composed, D glances over his shoulder too, and Bax heads in. Every hair on my arms stands up as he sits down in a chair across from the girl in my clothes, our cups from Lush Crush in plain sight next to her.

I drag my hand from my nose to my mouth as caustic unease burns all of me.

"Yeah," I say again.

D points toward the stairs, but I go around them and he follows me to the office. Standing aside once more, I let him enter first and when I don't close the door, the volume of the television goes up in the living room.

Everything behind my ribs pounds against impatience.

"So," my partner says, his tone low but casual as he drops all his weight into an oversized office chair and spins once. "Here we are."

Making myself lean against the desk that's next to him, I

cross my arms.

"Where?" I ask.

He smirks.

"A little past the point of no return, don't you think?"

Picking up a tennis ball from my desk, he passes it back and forth between his hands.

"This can't just go on," he says.

Like it's simple.

I shrug.

"We got shit to do, man," he continues.

Like I don't know.

"A business."

Like I forgot.

"I mean, it's not like you can take her with you to Philly tomorrow."

"Alright," I bite, shrugging again while the distance between me and my fall grows exponentially more intolerable. "What do we do?"

He tosses the ball in the air, catching it before he speaks.

"Bax is going to handle it."

Snorting, I stand up straight as offense and disbelief so jarring, so far out of the realm of possibility crash into me.

"You know what we're looking at," D says to my back, as I face books instead of him.

My head reels, and I stare blindly through spines, stuck on the slack in his.

"I mean, we've done some fucked-up shit before," he says. "But we'll rot for this."

*This*, he says.

Like she's not even a person.

"Look, Bax knows what he's doing," D says, dropping his voice lower. "He took care of everything in Pompano."

Fuck ups we've never spoken of freeze my vertebrae and turn my blood to cold water as I face my boy again. Laid back and passing the ball between his hands again, he meets my eyes.

"You dropped this girl on me," I remind him.

"Yeah," he says, sniffing. "And you brought her here."

"This isn't Bax's deal."

Moscow splits a smile, and I've known him long enough to know he's feigning just as much calm indifference as I am.

"What, you fucking got it for the kid now?"

There's a flicker in his dilated eyes as he asks it, a crack.

I lock on.

"Have I ever let you down?" I ask back, dropping my tone and digging in. "How much shit have I taken care of?"

Silent, the confidence and certainty this crook came here with subsides.

I grave my voice.

"How much have I fucking buried?"

Searching my eyes before finally dropping his, D chucks the ball back up.

"Alright," he says, half-spinning and catching it, tossing it to me as he stands. He pats my back. "You've got this."

He walks out, and everything in and around me dips like motion sickness at the drop in pressure.

Tossing the ball in the chair, I follow him, and Bax stands as we return.

Still where I left her, truly terrified watches me with glassy wide eyes as I look away.

My best friend for more than a decade drops his shades.

"I'll see you tomorrow." Cockiness returns, swerving his grin as I nod, and when Bax drops his palm for mine, I give it.

"See you, brother," he says.

I shake his hand, and the floor rocks beneath my feet. Dark eyes burn up my back as I close the door and as I watch them leave, gravity tilts and the atmosphere lurches.

I barely have shit locked up before I'm walking past her, stepping ahead of myself.

Short on balance, I brace my weight over the kitchen sink, and squeeze my eyes shut against the headache knotting my stomach. Loaded heat pulls like stones from my hips, and I feel like I can't see or breathe.

Leaning into my left hand, I unbuckle and unbutton with my right, disarming and dropping both nines in their holsters to the counter pushing them away.

Dark blurs as lightness floods me.

My chest heaves and my eardrums overflow, drowning me in the downpour. I bank myself against the sink and line my feet under my shoulders for stability, but it's not enough.

Turning on the tap and reaching for soap, I scrub my hands and wrists, between my fingers and under my nails while I strain to clear my vision. I focus on the feel of the water on my skin and the static sound of it running, but it's like I'm reeling in a tunnel.

Dropping my head and wiping my eyes in the arm of my shirt, and I try to breathe evenly.

But everything's fucked.

While chills creep and sweat beads too quickly, brave fingers brush the sides of my waist, taking me by surprise. My hands drip warm water as I instinctively catch smaller ones before they get too close to loaded weapons.

But I remember they're on the counter.

And she wraps her arms around me, gripping desperately.

My heart caves in, and her cry, muffled into my back, cuts clean through everything.

Storm-pressure in my ears splits around the broken sound, and I reach forward to shut the faucet off. Turning, I cup her face with wet hands, but before I can find her eyes, she pulls at my shirt, and I gather wholly vulnerable to myself unconditionally.

Shorter than me, her heart beats against my stomach, and she clings without reservation.

"Are you okay?" I ask, bending my knees and turning her face up from my chest.

Fear-filled, all-pupil eyes find mine as lamb nods, but she shakes. She blinks as I brush damp thumbs across her cheeks, and heavy tears fall fast. My forehead drops to hers, and shattered-small breaths wash over me with the scent of wedding cake and a current of terrified trust.

"Please—" It's a gasp she can't catch. "Don't let me go—"

Shaking my head, I collect her hands and bring them to my chest to tuck her completely between my arms as I brush her hair back, making sure each one is unharmed. My nose brushes hers, heated and cry-pink, as I tilt her face back toward mine, seeking to reassure her.

But dropped on me and mine to fall for clings to fistfuls of my tee shirt.

And as she blinks black lashes open for me, gravity settles

down.

Touching tear-cornered lips with my own follows naturally, and when she opens, tension pours into passionate protection, consuming and opening deeper as I bring her more near, almost losing my footing pressing myself closer.

We stumble, but don't fall as soft fingertips brush my neck, and my hands find the backs of her thighs. Kissing just like she laughs: honest, heartfelt and heartful, she pulls me down as I lift her up, and the hum she gives when my tongue finds hers makes every one of my nerves fire.

Seeking sanctuary there, I part her mouth more with my own, and she welcomes me into an even higher hum, slick warmth, eager sincerity. My pulse pounds as we kiss deeper, and when I feel her little weight press where my belt sits unbuckled and precaution no longer rests, hardened devotion fills me.

It takes a few beats to realize we're moving, and when I do, we're already halfway through the living room and approaching the stairs. I try to watch my steps as she whispers parted lips from my jaw to my neck, but her hands are in my hair, and preciousness worth everything rises into every kiss.

Overwhelmed like I've never known, I stop once halfway up the stairs, and again at the top of them, just to turn and press small and irreplaceable against the wall for balance while I give in to her so-open mouth.

I secure her to myself as I step inside my bright with daylight room, and when I kick the door closed, she wraps her arms around me and lifts in mine. She cups my cheeks, kissing me like I'm hers to keep, and it draws defenselessness from between my lungs. Humming in helpless harmony, her heart soars against my chest, and flutters everywhere my hands go, making me ache to give her everything.

She grips tighter to me as I cross my room, and I hold her close as I bend my knees at the edge of my bed. Her legs go slack when I lay her in the safest place I have, but unshy fingers remain in my hair as I come down above her.

Like they're what's holding me here.

Like I could bear to uncover her now.

With lips to urgently more and more open lips, I press unarmed hips into softer ones, and I love how she curves.

The littlest note enfolds me and melts between us as my undone buckle digs against her, and I lift to tug my belt away. The girl I picked up, fucked-up, and couldn't put on a bus comes into focus in the bit of distance, and I slip my hand under my shirt—the one she's wearing—over the bottom of her stomach, looking up when she inhales at new contact.

My heart rushes hard for eyes that are tearless and dilated wide even as sunlight pours in, showing me cheeks that are heated pink for a different reason now and lips that are swollen from moving with my own. Her chest and stomach rise and fall under black cotton, and I want this to stay with me forever too, to always remember the sight and sound and feel of her lifting from unmade stars, into my hand.

But her legs bend around me.

And my mouth returns to hers.

Feeling my way up her side, unable to touch her enough, pure tenderness enfolds me as I come back down. Under her blush and between shared breaths, soft in her sounds and bare in her eyes, innocence is as downright and all over this ransom as I am. It's strong in the unlearned way she curves and clings, and unmistakable in the shamelessly open way she kisses. It's inborn and sweetly-safe inside her, and not like anything I've ever admired or been a part of before.

Little untouched sighs as I kiss from her lips to her cheek, letting her breathe, but lifting from the rest of her is impossible. I keep how hard I am carefully away, lower than she is in my bed as I slide my palm further up her side. Brushing my thumb over the top of her ribcage, I bring her more to myself as my nose goes under her ear, into her hairline. I breathe her deeply, and she tilts back while my heart floods hard beats for vanilla flowers in the woods at night—my scent all over her—so good, my hips roll into the space between us.

Filling my room with the most doting note, in the pink up to her ears and lush behind them wraps her arms and legs tighter around me, and I kiss her.

Right there.

At the top of her neck, where our scent is richest.

I kiss her with lips and teeth and tongue like she's mine.

And she bares herself up to me.

Like she wants to be.

Pulling my collar away from her neck, I kiss across her shoulder, and tug the fabric down to kiss the top of her chest. I slide my other hand over her stomach, loving warm and silk-soft skin, and the dip of her belly button, and the way she can't finish any of her breaths as I kiss down, over my shirt on her and then under it. Pushing black cotton up to her ribs with my nose, I open and close my lips from her left side to her right, turning her with my hands. I kiss the curve I fell for this morning, and when I dip the tips of my fingers into the top of my sweats, inching them down only a bit, just enough to kiss her naked hip, lamb closes her eyes like she could die.

Half coming up, half dragging her down, I give my mouth to hers again, and she rises, kissing me like it's been forever. She pushes my shirt up too, and our stomachs touch as we fall into the flow together, and kiss closer, deeper, until it feels like instinct could kill me.

It throttles my lungs when I feel her hands go between us, untying grey cotton drawstrings and going for the zipper on my already unbuttoned jeans, but I reach between us too. Shaking my head as I part our lips, my pulse throbs painfully as I take her hands one by one in mine away from where my body aches toward hers with every heartbeat. I bring them to the back of my neck, while my eyes squeeze closed through need.

With her legs still around me, I come up, watching low-lidded dark eyes open to mine as I lift her hips to my own, and let her feel all of my want.

Wrapped in the warm, slow breath of unrestricted trust melting around and into me, I fall back above her, and steady myself with my hand over her shoulder. She goes totally soft for full contact, legs I love the feel of around my sides parting further as I press closer, and every one of my muscles tightens. Every synapse I'm made of fires, heavy with the pull toward where she's heartachingly delicate and open-unbroken.

Resting my forehead on hers, and my parted lips over a cupid's bow I made out on her first night here, I rock slowly forward, and feel my movement overwhelm her everywhere.

"Like this," I tell her, sliding my hand under the small of her back and bringing her up, into me as I roll my hips into hers again.

Already so furrowed brows dig closer together under mine, while black lashes flutter lowly, and her breath catches tight in her throat. Licking my lips over hers, I deliver her air with another slow pulse of my hips, and her eyes lilt closed.

"There you go," I whisper, loving that lids weighted by her own need ruffle and flitter for my voice. "Just like that."

Pressing deeper against chaste and more cherished than I knew, I open a deliberate rhythm, gradual and steadfast, and I swear her belly dips under mine. She shifts her grip to my shoulders, and feeling her hold onto me like this validates and gratifies on every level. Euphoria and yearning that are more than physical flare purely through me as I turn my head, kissing faded-pink red marks on her arm and matching ones on her wrist.

Even as cotton and denim remain between us, I roll heavy pressure where she needs me most at a pace that makes her breaths shake.

That's where her first little fire starts.

Right between her lungs.

Bringing her closer by the small of a back that almost knocked me to my knees, I offer her all that I am with intentionally deeper movements. Her chin and bottom lip quiver around laid-bare sounds, and I brush my parted mouth over hers, enamored as the same shaking spreads down through both her legs, into how she lifts and clings, and it's all I can do to open my eyes.

Burning bright sunlight shines across everything I want to sink inside, as I lean up to witness every precious rise and flutter and flame of first time fulfillment. Her whole body moves with my cadence, and unashamed pleas slip and drift as I lead her further than she's ever gone, and more near to me than anything.

"Right here," I whisper, wanting her eyes as tender trembling I'm chasing finds hips that I'm guiding, and her mouth falls slack.

Gravity and reason open, showing me all her vulnerability, and I lay down persistent intent she can't get enough of. With my shirt still pushed up, her bare stomach quakes under mine, and I gather her to every beat and pulse and push, showing her exactly what she's like.

"Right here, baby," I say again, the corners of my lips curving as needy whimpers break into pretty cries.

And her eyes close.

And I moan against her cheek because—

There's nowhere she doesn't shake.

And there's nowhere I don't feel it.

Helpless and irresistible, lamb lifts from my bed as she comes, and I kiss down to her neck, carrying her though.

I kiss down her chest, tracing the curves of her breasts through my shirt, brushing lips and breath over nipples that are hard beneath black cotton. I kiss between them, where her wild heart pounds, and I close my eyes, wrapped and warm in brand-new beats and sun-outlined heights I wouldn't trade for anything. Her chest heaves with all her gentle strength, and the sound I want to go down forever in fills my ears.

A little rough from all her gasping, her laugh is entirely enamoring, and it makes me smile so fucking hard.

Lifting, I find dark eyes lit-up and waiting for mine, and my chest swells around undeniable pride. Her giggle grows and her

# a story about falling by Sarah

fingers fall from my hair, toward her mouth, but I shake my head and bring my lips to hers before she can cover them.

Forehead to forehead, I hold her smile open with my own, and let the sound I want always surrounded in fill my room, until the girl giving it to me is all soft touches and looks that feel like becoming.

Listening to her breathe, I watch her eyes watch mine as I rejoin our hips, and she welcomes all of my aching need with warmth twice as ardent as before. We start slower this time, and my point of no return holds me with a force I couldn't fight even if I wanted to, drawing intuition from my hips like there's nothing more natural in the world.

I give it to her until small shakes diffuse back out into her laugh, and I carry her through again, openly committing her softest sounds to a place deeper than memory.

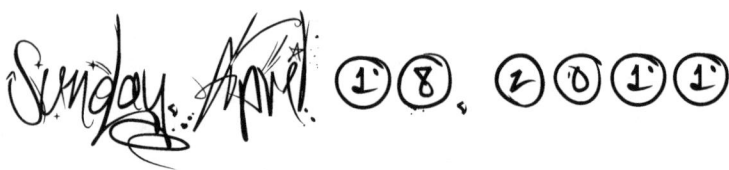

# 3:37 pm

The slightest shift pulls me from deep sleep, and I know I'm too light before I even open my eyes. Adrenaline swallows me, and my hand flies to my hip.

In the split second waking takes, my pulse pounds panic.

But then I see her.

I feel her.

And remember.

I relax around the girl nestled to my chest, and it takes a minute for my heart to slow down, but lamb hardly stirs in my anxiousness. She breathes evenly and effortlessly against me, and I love the way her hand looks on my sternum.

But I want insurance within reach.

I kiss her cheek, and when she still doesn't wake, I get up with a smile I can't fight.

Because I did that.

112

# a story about falling by Sarah

I gave that reprieve.

Buttoning back up in afternoon sunlight, I pop a Jolly Rancher and head downstairs to find Lydie and Denise still in their pajamas, stretched out on the living room floor and laughing at a movie. Two pizza boxes sit on the coffee table behind them, and my smile grows a little more, thankful for the late delivery and their sleeping in through everything else.

"Good morning, darling," Lyd teases, her playful good nature wide awake as I pass them.

"Morning," I answer easily, heading to the kitchen.

Everything in me that's easy shifts as I turn the corner.

They're what I came down for, and right where I left them, but just the sight of my guns brings all that's fucked rushing back to the surface. Heavy as they are in my hands as I pick them up, they're warranted.

Back upstairs, mine to save is curled contently in my bed, and even as worries creep back into place, the sight of her there both calms and emboldens me.

Closing my door, I set both holsters on the nightstand and step out of Vans I fell asleep in before getting back beside her.

Stretching a little and reaching for me as I return her to myself, lamb yawns. She hums when I enfold her in both arms, moving my hand through her hair and brushing my nose along her crown. My scent on her is stronger than before, and softened at the same time by new lushness in hers. She smells intimate and sweet, familiar and personal to me, and I draw an indulgent breath to my chest.

"Where'd you go?" she asks softly, sounding only half-awake.

Deeply, my heart beats.

"Just to the kitchen."

Entangling herself around me with eyes closed, lamb presses her chest to mine and buries her face in my neck. She brushes her nose across my skin as she breathes in too, and I lay my head down, held and holding while she falls back asleep.

I close my eyes, but tomorrow bears down on me.

The unpredictability of what's to come harrows me out with all that's passed, and I lie awake between Violet saying *Rhys is here*, and D telling me to *roll up*, and is all of this what friendship is?

*She's not a hostage.*

*It gets the job done.*

*You can lock me in here.*

*Did you suddenly forget how, too?*

My chest caves in around the memory of pretty, carefree lashes, and I gather the girl I could have driven right past, even more near.

She pulls me closer, and it takes a while, but I don't feel myself fall asleep.

The sun's starting to set the next time I open my eyes, waking to the sound of hunger.

"I'm starving," sleepy-voiced and face to face with me on my pillows says, smiling shyly while her stomach grumbles.

Under black cotton at the small of her back, I brush my thumb along one of her dimples.

"I told you snow cones don't count as breakfast."

Burying a light laugh in the bend of my elbow, she closes her eyes and kisses me there.

"There's pizza downstairs," I tell her, running my nose and

lips along her temple, more than content to stay right here. "Lyd and Denise are up."

She clings like she wants to stay too, but her stomach speaks out again, louder this time, and she presses gently down on me for balance as she gets up. I stand behind her, and as she yawns again and ties grey drawstrings, my eyes go to my nightstand.

I don't want to call her fear back, but protecting her is paramount now.

Unholstering one of the 19s, I lift my shirt and tuck it into the front of my jeans. Dreamy smile corners tighten a little as we head out of my room, but a few steps into the hallway, she takes my hand.

Made-tenacious, my heart beats.

Lydie and her girl join us in the kitchen. The three of them take seats at the table around reheated pizza while unable to sit, I eat a piece standing up, to the left of what nothing can make me back down from now.

Grabbing a bottle of water and passing one to my girl, I eat another piece and finish what she can't. Conversation flows easily between her and Lyd while the sun dips lower in the sky, streaming burning orange hues through patio doors. Locusts and crickets buzz outside while cars go by, and the sprinklers in the backyard kick on. I can faintly hear one of my neighbors mowing his lawn, and for all its fucked-up reality, everything feels normal and perfect for a second, like life is just like this.

Going on.

I trade water for cold beer, and share it with my reason to stand up straight.

Leaning back in her chair, stretching her arms like she's fully satisfied, she lifts her hair off her back and neck like she wants to pull it up. Denise passes her a ponytail holder from her wrist, and while lamb gathers messy between first and second base waves up onto her crown, I notice the purple-red mark behind her ear, right below her hairline.

I have to pocket my free hand just to keep from reaching out—I want to touch it so badly.

They talk a little more while my heart beats, purposeful and resolute, until she turns my way.

Giving me sweetheart eyes over a thankful smile, she blinks, naturally at first, then intentionally-coyly batting dark lashes until I can't fight my grin.

Like fucking crazy, my heart beats.

"You good?" I ask, already knowing.

"Mhmm."

She nods, pressing together lips I know the feel and taste and weight of.

I tilt my head toward the stairs.

"Come on."

She tugs on my fingers at the top of them, flocking to me, and I turn her around the corner. Holding her hands in mine to ensure her safety, I kiss her in the same place I stopped this afternoon. It's softer this time, slower, but no less binding.

Unselfish-hearted and eye-level with my own rocks to her tiptoes.

"You taste like Red Sky and prosciutto," she teases.

Grinning, I kiss her again.

Back behind my closed door, sitting on the bathroom counter after she brushes her teeth, she swings her feet while I

# a story about falling by Sarah

brush mine.

"I have a really weird confession," she warns as I rinse.

"Okay," I say so she'll continue. "Let's hear your really weird confession."

Smiling without hiding it, she meets my eyes, and there's no pressure or weight here.

Nothing hurts, and nothing conflicts.

"I have a really big crush," she says so seriously. "On your toothbrush."

I laugh from all the way down, so deep I feel it between all my ribs.

Stepping out for clean clothes, I head back to shower while she thumbs through my music.

Alone with thoughts that crowd and goad in her absence, I don't take my time. I wash clean with the same soap and shampoo as the girl in my room and when I turn the water off, the wispy opening notes of *In A Safe Place* filter through the wall.

Drying off, I pull on boxers and old cut-off sweats, a clean crew neck, and I wipe some steam away from the mirror.

Better rested than the last time I looked, I shake wet hair out with my fingers. Hazel-flecked blue eyes reflect stubble over a no longer so-smooth shave and a cut above my brow that's another day closer to healed. Leaving it un-bandaged and my gun on the counter, I open the door thinking I'll find lamb in my bed.

And I do.

But not how I expect.

Sitting in the very center of my sheets, lit only by the last rays of sunset, compellingly precious is bare shouldered under my flag, and has it held to her chest. All of her hair's still up, showing

117

me her naked neck, and as melodic tones melt into a magnetic tempo, she looks at me with eyes as gleaming as her skin.

Captivated, my heart beats.

Her teeth flash as her smile parts, and she ducks a little, just for a second, before looking up again, and I approach her like the innocent she is.

Fragile.

Tempting.

Powerful.

Holding glistening dark eyes as I reach the bed, I drop my knees to it, and baby to me leans back as I lean forward, into gravity and onto my hands. Breaths tinted with my Crest pick up as I crawl over her, and old stars dip down a little as she reaches for me. Brave but tentative, her fingers find my unarmed sides as I linger above, overwhelmed and filling my senses with the sight and scent and sound of her boldness.

"Can I?" she asks, brushing her touch through my shirt when I don't catch her hands.

The corners of my lips pull with consent, and she tugs up the shirt I just put on while I let down her hair. She goes for my chest, and everything that follows just flows.

Turning and shifting and kissing, I join her under my flag, bringing it over both of us as I take my place over surrendered and soft, keeping her bare skin from rising city lights, the darkness of night, and everything that isn't me. She makes me hard, and I make her shake, and by the time moonlight's filling my room, so are her prettiest sounds, and I'm shaking too.

With her back to my chest, safe-kept under faded soft canvas, lamb sleeps with both of her hands over my right, between

a story about falling by Sarah

her legs. Pressed deeply and carefully inside where she's most delicate, my curved middle finger holds her open and to me all through the night.

The slightest shifts—a yawn, a tiny flex of muscles, my breath along her ear—draw supple circles from her hips, and she wakes countless times, coming and needing to come.

Too into her to sleep, I learn this person by heart.

My chest brims against her shoulders while she sleepy-stirs in the still-dark morning, waking soaked and soft and open like a flame. She rocks sweetly against my unabridged touch, but whimpers like she can't, and I bring my other hand underneath both of hers, coaxing and adoring little yearning with both of my own.

Heartened beneath the stars, she unravels in my arms, desperate whimpers melting into affectionate pleas as I guide dizzy dips and helpless tilts toward shakes she can't resist.

"Stay with me," I whisper with my voice as much as my touch. "Here, right here, baby."

Using my nose to nudge her hair back from her neck, I find a mark made for significance-found instead of control-lost, and kiss it with warm breath and parted lips as she finds another peak.

I realize as I take her where she needs to go, that's it.

While tired, touch-tipsy and tender in a brand new way drifts in my arms, I know that as much as I want all of this resolved, there's no solution here.

And no possibility for it.

But we don't have to stay here.

The same feeling from yesterday morning, when we got

in the car and my gut kicked me to just go, hits me again, it's exponentially stronger now.

D was right.

We do have a business, but my best friend's hand doesn't feed me.

We feed each other.

It's always been that way.

And sometimes, businesses fall apart.

Just like friendships.

Broken, but in the right place, my heart beats.

And I can't wait another second.

Kissing her soft crown and careful with my touch, I turn my future to face me. She hums in my arms, and I brush my fingers between strong, small shoulders, waking her while it's still dark out.

Lamb smiles as her lashes lift, and the whites of her eyes glow around dreamy, faith-filled irises.

"Hey," she whispers, touching my cheek.

I wish I could let her sleep.

I wish I'd realized all of this sooner.

I wish we could stay here, this way.

But it's Monday.

The flower girls won't be at the house until after ten, and I don't usually meet Moscow until eleven, but I want to be way out of town by then.

We have to move.

And it has to be now.

"Hey." Closing my hand over hers, I bring her palm to my lips.

# a story about falling by Sarah

"Hey," she says again, beaming even in shadows.

I kiss the heel of her hand.

"Let's get out of here."

Little brows furrow while her smile grows.

"You want to go get breakfast and watch the sun rise?"

There's teasing in her voice, but I know she'd love it, and it makes me want to give it to her. I laugh a little at her question, but in the back of my mind, I make plans to.

"No." My mouth is suddenly dry. "I mean like, out of here."

Confusion narrows dark eyes as she searches mine, and my pulse thumps against the base of my skull, out into my eardrums and down against my lungs. I feel it everywhere, pushing me, and I'm reminded of trying to put this girl on a bus to save herself.

But this is different.

"You and me," I say.

She blinks, and nothing compares to the pure possibility that flashes in her eyes. Open and infinite, overwhelmed but unafraid, imagination and abandon all flicker together. But in the next second, a wince tightens her features, and as she bites into her bottom lip, I know she's thinking of all we'll leave behind.

I am too.

We could come back.

Eventually.

Maybe.

After Dolzhikov and Rhys sort each other out.

But I know how that ends.

And the choice I'm making will leave no room for forgiveness.

Boundless eyes close, and tears slip as I gather my choice. There's so much she could ask, about her parents, and where, and how long, but a deeper drive, the strength and courage that the will to live and let live takes, endures. I stroke her back, and she nods after a few breaths, exhaling and looking up at me with the bravest eyes I've ever seen.

We move swiftly.

I dress first, and then while she does, I head downstairs.

Collecting folders and savings I keep in the basement, I pull the My Thai take-out menu off the fridge and write account numbers and combinations down on the back of it for Lyd. There's more than enough saved up downstairs to cover everything she could need, but that doesn't make writing my goodbye any easier.

Grieving at the kitchen table, my heart beats.

Back upstairs, lamb's got her boots on. Minus sheer black stockings and plus the white tee she pulled off me last night, she's back in her denim cutoffs. Sitting on the edge of my bed, she holds my hoodie in her lap and my flag is folded next to her, under my toothbrush.

It splits heaviness in my chest and reminds me what this is all for. Reason and relief shape my lips up, and she stands.

"I didn't know if you'd want to take anything," she says, making her way to me with a smile that assures just as it seeks assurance. "But I've collected the bare essentials."

I put both hands on everything I care to take and bring her to me by her hips. Dark blue before-dawn light glows through my windows, and I give her the softest kiss.

Pocketing my wallet, I think about Sonny as I grab my phone.

All heart all along may fuck around, but my oldest friend has always had his head on straight, and it hurts, but I don't text him. There's nothing tangible connecting him to what we've done, or where we're going, and it should stay that way.

While my girl pulls my hoodie over her head, I strap protection in place. Grabbing my flag and toothbrush in one hand, she holds her other out, and I take it as I look around my room for what could be the last time.

Palm to palm with something no amount of money could buy, it's easy to leave all that I own behind.

Lighter shades of blue streak the sky as we head outside, and as I close her into the '65 and come around to my side, burning neural energy courses through me.

Not fear, or pressure, or frustration, it's closer to that rush I get every time Barlow brings his blade to my neck, like the influx of purpose and intuition when I gather lamb to myself.

Sitting down next to her in my car, I feel entirely and intensely alive, and as I drive, the feeling only increases.

Heading south, I stop only to fill up the tank and top off fluids. It's about seven hours to the border, and I'll have to set her up first, but I want to make it at least to Erie. New paperwork will take a day at least, and I have friends there we can stay with.

In the car again, quiet on my right turns on the radio and twists the dial until she finds catchy-deep lo-fi beats that make everything feel real.

Still too early for the daily rise and grind, the streets are mostly empty save for big rigs and the occasional cop car. I roll down my window to let fresh air in, and as we merge onto I-70, my girl faces me.

"So," she starts. "Where are we going?"

I glance over, and the first rays of sunlight peek through cloudy blue.

"Where do you want to go?"

She shrugs.

"I don't know. Canada?"

I smile.

"I don't have a passport though," she tells me.

Left hand on the wheel, I reach with my right and bring runaway fingers to my lips.

"I know."

Exiting onto 29 South, I graze my teeth over little knuckles and hear her smile.

"I have some money in a house, in Gaithersburg," I tell her. "We just have to pick it up."

Nodding, she turns bare knees toward me.

"Can we get food after that?" she asks softly.

I grin against her hand.

"What, you want to get breakfast and watch the sun rise?"

She glows good morning vibes.

"Only if breakfast consists of biscuits and gravy," she says. "All the gravy. And sausage. And bacon."

Totally hers, my heart beats.

"I'm going to get the biggest glass of milk in the history of glasses of milk."

There's playfulness in her voice, excitement, and I know it won't all be like this.

It'll hurt too.

But she'll live.

"And an orange juice," she adds, leaning back. Laying her head on the seat and her right arm over her stomach, little lionhearted inhales all the way deep, and hums when she lets it go.

# a story about falling by Sarah

Moving in and out of clouds, the sun climbs slowly higher as miles pass and disquiet escalates inside me.

The driveway's empty as we approach the house with a couple hours to spare, but it doesn't do much for my nerves.

It shouldn't end like this.

But D's leaving me without a choice.

What I need to take care of lamb is in this house, and it's mine.

Rightfully.

I'm the one crossing state lines with a full trunk twice a week.

I'm the one making dirty cash clean at Six Sheets.

And if D would let her go, I'll be the one taking a hostage off his hands.

I earn more than my share in what we do.

But despite all this, there's no part of me that thinks he'll see it that way.

That's why we're here before even the starlings in the beech trees are up, and why I didn't leave my reason for being here at my place, even though I could have done this faster without her. It's why I don't stop her when she gets out at the same time I do.

I don't want to bring her inside.

But by my side is the only place I know for sure she's safe.

I keep my pace steady as we head to the door, not wanting to startle her, I keep my pace steady as we head to the door, but once it's closed behind us, nerves that are already firing on high alert double up. Everything in me quickens, and it doesn't go unnoticed.

"What?" she asks as I grab her hand. "What's wrong?"

"Come on."

Leading her downstairs, I don't let go until I have to open the floor safe. Turning the dial and opening heavy steel finds my duffel next to Moscow's, and unzipping black canvas reveals every stack in its right place.

Closing up and standing straight, I sling the burden of escape over my shoulder as I take my girl's hand back in mine. Up old stairs and into a kitchen lit with morning, we're almost to the living room when I hear a car outside.

The drop in my chest is unlike anything.

It's not the rumble of Moscow's SS, but it doesn't matter who it is.

Tearing bare panic, my heart beats, and I pull first and foremost instinctively behind me.

Momentarily frozen, I sweat bullets while everything under my skin tenses with the basic impulse to protect and survive. Reason worth all her weight grips onto me with everything she has, and all her hopes, big and small, fall on my back.

Digging courage from a place I didn't know I had, I move my feet toward the back door, because I'm getting her out of this house.

Out of Baltimore.

This girl's going to Brown.

We're going to watch the sun rise.

And I'm going to get her the biggest glass of milk in—

The front door opens.

"Stay with me," I urge her, bending my knees and moving quieter.

Loaded, my heart beats.

But drugs are quicker than blood.

# a story about falling by Sarah

And *this* is the thing about finding a maniac.

He finds you.

In true Rhys form, bullshit that started all of this sways on shifty feet in the back doorway, here when he shouldn't be, and dirtier than I've ever seen him. Hood up and piece in his hand, lamb's brother is beyond spun, and I don't want to do this in front of her.

But I'll do what I have to.

Halted in my tracks, keeping innocence tucked behind me, I square my shoulders as my pulse races with knowing that if he's here, someone else came through the front door.

I don't reach for my gun. Not yet. This guy's too volatile.

"What are *you* doing here?" he asks, eyes darker than his sister's and totally empty as he sizes up the situation. "Kenny? What the fuck's going on?"

Quick footsteps approach from behind, and I recognize her voice, but Rhys is so jumpy he points his heat at his own girl.

"He's not in the basement—"

The shot he fires is loud in the house, rattled worse with his scream and hers, and the one that rips between my shoulders. Ringing deafness fills my ears for a beat, but it's the distraction we need.

And I run with it.

Sunlight hits everywhere as we bolt out the back door. With lamb in tow, I make the straightest line possible toward my car, and my pulse pounds so-close hope.

But as we turn the corner and the front end of my Buick comes into view, so does the Impala.

And everything bottoms out.

Hands in his pockets and as blond as the sun coming through the trees, Moscow stands beside his car. Sunglasses hide his eyes, but I don't have to see them to know he's higher than the sky. It's the nonchalance in his posture and redness in his nose.

Smirking, he sniffs as he sees us, and it isn't because he's about to cry.

"You know," D says, un-pocketing his hands to rub the back of his head. "If someone had asked me this time yesterday, who's the one person in the world you can bet your life on, I'd have said you."

Between lungs too tight to breathe, my heart beats.

"But then I saw you with her."

Still-fresh resentment bites his tongue and I see him under his shades, looking at the duffel on my arm and skittish Doc Martens hiding behind my Vans.

My betrayed best friend shakes his head.

"I mean, how far back do we go?" he asks, knowing the answer. "A decade? Simon Pilkington? We came up from nothing. You and me." He points as he paces, and resentment in his voice breaks around truth. "I gave Lyd my fucking bone marrow, and you're taking this motherfucker's little sister out for fucking snow cones?"

Securing lamb behind my back, I stand all the way straight and drop my bag.

D can have it.

He could have it all.

But he doesn't care.

The nearness of my car pulls at me, and my heart fucking beats.

# a story about falling by Sarah

"You know," he starts again, his voice thin. "You know where this gets me, CL?"

Nudging the only soft part of any of this back, toward the Buick, I keep my right hand ready at my side.

D pats his chest, over his heart.

"Right fucking here."

Drawing from my hip, I push lamb toward safety.

"Run—"

But I'm too late.

Her scream is louder than my boy's shot, and hurts a thousand times more than the hole in my chest.

I'm vaguely aware of other shots, but I'm falling.

I'm on the ground, and I'm still falling.

Lamb's hands are on my face, but she's staring at my chest. I can feel pain pouring out of me and the world coming apart, but all I want are her eyes.

They open and cry as I touch her cheek, and given to meaning, my heart beats.

"No," she begs, shaking her head. "No, no, no, please, no."

Warm and comforting, I feel her hands, pressing where it hurts the most.

And then—

I can't.

Black creeps around the edges of my vision, and I open my eyes wide, but it doesn't clear.

It grows.

Blocking the sun, silhouetted in its shine, inevitability with dark eyes that are with me for life weeps, but she's alive.

I can see her looking at me.

129

And then, I can't.

"Please, no, please. Stay with me, please, please, CL, please …"

Softly running out, I hear her cries.

Until I can't.

And I'm scared.

Directly in front of me in a dirty little parking lot, with lamb smiling up as I drop my hood from her crown and cover her in light, my heart beats in the dark.

Desperate and ungentle against the coming quiet, it fights.

And burns.

And beats.

And beast …

Then doesn't.

## 7:48 pm

itting down and starting is always hard, because it means facing it.

And tonight, that feels impossible.

But I know it will make me feel closer to courage.

So when I can't sit down, I write standing up.

*Dear CL,*

And when it's too much to look at, I write with eyes closed.

*I graduated today.*

*I wished you were there.*

*I wish you were here.*

*And I know I write that every time, but I don't think you mind.*

Pausing to wipe tears on black cotton sleeves that still smell a little like his smoke and soap and a shared orange, I blink a few times and start again.

*Mom's still trying to change my mind about Brown. She loves*

131

*that I got into the program, but she doesn't love that it's six hours away. She wants me to choose a school closer to home.*

*Who can blame her, right?*

*They threw me a party. There's a cake and all this food, and a banner with my name on it, but I kind of really hate it. It doesn't feel like me.*

*Sonny and Lyd still call me lamb, and I love it even though it hurts.*

*They came today. They're downstairs with everyone else, and it's good to have them here—*

I break down around a sob I can't swallow.

*But I needed you for a minute, and then I got up here and I couldn't even sit down, and now I can't stop crying.*

Sinking to the floor against my bed, I focus on my breathing until I can see clearly.

*Remember in your room, when you asked me if I was writing a book?*

*I wasn't. I just wanted to know about you. I still want to know about you. Sonny tells me things, and I always want more, but I get scared to ask because what if he tells me everything? What if I run out of pieces of you? So I try to only ask when I really need it, but it's hard because I always really need it.*

*Anyway.*

*These letters feel like that sometimes. They were my counselor's idea, but I feel I'm writing a book I never wanted to, full of all these things I'd be really okay without, and I wish I could give it a different beginning, and what if it never ends? What if I always have to leave parties to come feel close to you? What if I write this book for the rest of my life?*

132

# a story about falling by Sarah

*I miss you so much.*

*I wake up hearing your voice in the middle of the night, telling me to run. To stay with you. That now's a terrible time to forget again, and I try really hard to not just hurt, and it all just pulls in my chest, and I never know how I'm supposed to feel.*

*Sonny says that's okay.*

*He tells me not to be sad, because you'd do it again if you could, but that's not always easy either, and I know he gets sad too. He takes care of me, but sometimes when he calls, I know it's for him.*

*He misses you too.*

*It's really scary sometimes, but you did a good thing, and it feels safe to say that here.*

*Thank you.*

Closing wet eyes, I focus on my heart. It's broken-open and sore, but sometimes when I listen to it long enough, it steadies me.

Leaning my head back against stars and stripes, I let my breathing even out.

*Always,* I write.

*Lamb*

Gathering my overnight bag, I pack a toothbrush that's mine now and grab the notebook I just closed.

Just in case.

Downstairs, I thank Mom and Dad for my party, and for letting me go out tonight, and for everything. I know they worry, but after taking my freedom away led to a kidnapping, two funerals, and a son in prison, they also go easy, and they listen to me better than they ever have.

"Thank you," I say again, hugging my mom.

*Don't Let Me Go*

Comfort and companionship wait at the end of the driveway in a new Defender. Reaching over from the driver's seat, Sonny opens my door, and I get in next to the one person it feels okay to lean on.

As he pulls out onto the street, sunset light pours through the windshield, right into my eyes. Bright colors sting, but my broken heart warms under them, reminding me with each tender beat that I'm alive.

Rolling my window down, I let fresh air in, and when it feels good just to breathe, I don't fight it.

I smile.

*the end*

# Acknowledgments

To The Raveonettes, Daughter, Phantogram, Josh Record, Imaginary Friend, Eels, The Neighbourhood, The 1975, Johnny Cash, Sebadoh, The Album Leaf, Passenger, Arctic Monkeys, Nas, Damien Marley, Mike Mignola, Bill Finger and Bob Kane, John Romita, Sr, Gerry Conway, and Ross Andru, Mogwai, Mark Rothko, Mark Z. Danielewski, Nayyirah Waheed, Banksy, Pink Floyd, Hank Williams, Sam Cooke, Easy-E, Eminem, Elton John, Yoko Ono, The Beatles, Chuck Palahniuk, Andy Heyward, Jean Chalopin and Bruno Bianchi, L. Frank Baum, Donald Levine, Now, Now, Trailer Trash Tracys, Broods, Johnnyswim, The Wright Brothers, The Arctic Monkeys, The xx, Neil Young, Don DeLillo, and Liars, thank you for making art that speaks to my heart.

To Nicola, Pico, Jac, Erika, Peta, Mandy, Mollie, Stacey, Jamie, Sammi, AL, Riley, AnaLisbeth, Nic, Alex Owens, Sariedee, Nicole Andrew, Nicole Dowd, Nicole Hampson Loen, Amber Sachs, coldasnicole, tapenoon, Frenchie, Panda, Jannat, Natalee, Karla, Sofia Foster, Berta Moore, Sam Stettner, Tracy, Hadley, Robin, Paola, Ari, Tess, Palmerin, my mimosa, my carebear, thank all of you for all the ways you've been there for me and for love in my heart, not only for support, but for being sources of legit joy. I'm so thankful to and for all of you. I love you guys.

To a-double-a, thank you so much for letters I read more times than I can count. Your voice is not as small as you think. It picked me up more than a few times, and helped put this together into what it is now. It's part of this, and ransom thanks you too.

To Ernest, and to Ray, to Katy, Brenna, Aiden, John, Sherry, Heather, Frederico Suave, Dyan, David, Jordan, Emily, Amber, and Zero, thank you for making my on and off days better just by being a part of them. Little talks and laughing with you guys means more to me than maybe shows. I'm thankful to have you in my life. I love all of you.

Thank you, little darkling, for encouragement that lights me up, and for a friendship that means more to me all the time. Thank you for giving everything I write a chance, and for a hoodie I love, you know, the one that makes us triplets with the noodle. I can't wait to see you this summer! Hey, do you want a flower crown? I love you, Autumn.

Thank you, Coree, for years of closeness and inspiration. I miss, and look up to you so much. I'm so thankful to share life and art with you, be it in music, in words, talking of Michelangelo, forgetting my pants in the hallway, or in barrier-bruises I still miss. I'm thankful the youth has you to learn from. You're better than day-trips for a pain-fix and Bayside car rides with the windows down in the summer. I love you, KRG.

Thank you, brightheart, darling, poppypretty, for sharing my blood type and transfusions that were amazing motivation to my heart. Thank you for all caps excitement, and reminding me what makes this art, and to trust my guts. You bring my smile out every time we talk, and help me look up. You know. Toward the bright side. Thank you for nourishing me and so many loves in my heart, all the ways that you have. I cherish and admire, and love you so much, Michelle.

Thank you, bunny, for nights that get us away from everything else. You're someone I learn from, and with, and want to always know. Laughing with you, screaming in the thundering downpour, pancocks, flowers, aquariuseseseses, and guess who, and long talks in your car or over hot bread are some of my favorite things ever. Come over and make a cupcake mess in my kitchen. I love you, Pocahontas rib.

Thank you, Moses made of little blue flowers, who I hold in such high regard and so warmly in my heart. You're one of my favorite people in the whole world, and are inspiring to me on countless levels. Your backbone and tender heart assure, enliven, and revitalize my own consistently. I'm so proud of you every day. Thank you for being my family, and my friend of forever now. I'll never stop being so gratefully glad we ditched those boys for each other. I love you more than Bright Eyes birthday shows, I'm not even waiting, winged creatures, and puppy in a cup. I love you with all my heart, Birzer.

PS, hi, tot. Hi, little Olive. I love you guys so crazy much too.

Thank you so much, such a major crazy much, babyblue, for every last hour you have put into straightening this boy's suit and getting his hair right. For being the first (and only one, until right this second) one I wanted to tell when Sonny knocked me down and I stained State Avenue. Thank you for pictures that help me find my smile, and for sharing yours with me. Thank you for more prudent, more loving, more supportive care than anyone has ever put into my work. Your eyes must be so tired right now, but even as they are, I can feel your heart beating only love. Real, sincere, grateful, proud, unselfish, totally whole and endless and warmer than anything, love. There is no one who loves like you do. Thank you so much for believing in me, and being brave when I need you to bear with me. Thank you for feeding me, inside and out. Thank you for Simon Pilkington, and for this girl's crush. Thank you for writing on oranges and bubble tape to reach my heart, for putting flags together for me and taking all the photos, for sending me all the red Jolly Ranchers, and for voicenotes that I live on, and a hat that matches yours that I pretty much never take off lately. Thank you for ribbons I still tie on when I need to feel a little extra loved, even when I don't tell you about it. Thank you so much for finding all the question marks. You are my favorite place, my favorite sound, my good morning, my always and all ways, my partner, my shelter, my bio and summary expert, and the coolest person I know. My person. I love you more than books are good, more than our collective love for all the stars and all the flowers, and more than any distance could ever compete with. I love you, boo, baby, beloved to me, Karin. Je suis nee pour elle aimer.

To the little buffalo, fast asleep in my bed right now, thank you so much for keeping my feet warm as I work, and work. Thank you for kissing tears away, sharing your heartbeat when I'm scared, and for painted clouds. Thank for telling me all about it in the middle of the night, and for your morning dance, and for the way you welcome me every time I come home. I love you so much and so without any end, ever snow boots baby.

Sawyer, you're okay too. I guess. You know. For a floppy motherfucker. I love you, foofa-loofa.

Thank you, so much, so much, Bishop. You have let me type

pretty much every word of this story and all of this on your laptop, over and over again, and I'm so thankful that you have. Like, all the time. Thank you. Thank you for a home I feel at home in, for killing the spiders, for offering to save the whole document when it got corrupted last night. Thank you for mini-feasts, and for my old man sweater that I could live in, and for remembering corny jokes to tell me, because I love that so much. For Houston, because having you there is something I want to always remember, no matter how old or crazy I get. It's one of my favorite memories of my whole life. Thank you for drunk movie trips and for being someone I love to spend time with, for letters you sent to me while I was in Emporia, and for prank phone calls I'll never forget. I need bear assistance, and I can't wait to see Chuck Palahniuk with you! There is no one else in the whole world like you to me, no one else that could ever fill your place in my heart or life. You're my family, and my friend, and I would be so lost without you. I love you so much, dudeman.

And to the lion—

You are to me, like nothing I've ever written before. You helped me find new parts of my own heart, and trusted me with everything that meant the most to you. Thank you for that, and for the strength throughout all of this to do all that had to be done. Thank you for assurance, and for pulling the curtain, and for running with me, because I want to remember it forever, and thank you so much for not letting me go.

Right from the start.

Thank you for ransom. I love her, and I always will.

I love you.

# About Sarah

Love's listener is half sugar cookie, half wildfire. Currently based in Kansas City, where she dance-walks and shit-talks with a little buffalo by her side and her notebook never further than her fingertips, she prefers her coffee French-pressed and her apples Lady-Pink. She loves breaking rules, keeping secrets, working under the sunrise, and every star in the sky.

Hearts are her thing.

Sarah is the co-author of Dusty, and the sun half of Sparrow AuSoleil.

This is her first published solo effort.

## For more information on her past, present, and future work:

www.littlegreypages.tumblr.com
www.twitter.com/littlegreyache
www.facebook.com/littlegreyache
www.goodreads.com/littlegreyache
www.amazon.com/author/littlegreyache

43749451R00091

Made in the USA
San Bernardino, CA
26 December 2016